Talon pack ; bk. 6

P9-CQW-327

Destiny

Disgraced

A Talon Pack Novel

By
Carrie Ann Ryan

Henderson County Public Library

Destiny Disgraced copyright © 2017 Carrie Ann Ryan

All Rights Reserved

ISBN: 978-1-943123-60-5

Cover Art by Charity Hendry

This ebook is licensed for your personal enjoyment only.
This ebook may not be re-sold or given away to other
people. If you would like to share this book with another
person, please purchase an additional copy for each person
or use proper retail channels to lend a copy. If you're
reading this book and did not purchase it, or it was not
purchased for your use only, then please return it and
purchase your own copy. Thank you for respecting the hard
work of this author.
All characters in this book are fiction and figments of the
author's imagination.

Henderson County Public Library

Author Highlights

Praise for Carrie Ann Ryan....

"Carrie Ann Ryan knows how to pull your heartstrings and make your pulse pound! Her wonderful Redwood Pack series will draw you in and keep you reading long into the night. I can't wait to see what comes next with the new generation, the Talons. Keep them coming, Carrie Ann!" –Lara Adrian, New York Times bestselling author of CRAVE THE NIGHT

"Carrie Ann Ryan never fails to draw readers in with passion, raw sensuality, and characters that pop off the page. Any book by Carrie Ann is an absolute treat." – New York Times Bestselling Author J. Kenner

"With snarky humor, sizzling love scenes, and brilliant, imaginative worldbuilding, The Dante's Circle series reads as if Carrie Ann Ryan peeked at my personal wish list!" – NYT Bestselling Author, Larissa Ione

"Carrie Ann Ryan writes sexy shifters in a world full of passionate happily-ever-afters." – *New York Times* Bestselling Author Vivian Arend

"Carrie Ann's books are sexy with characters you can't help but love from page one. They are heat and heart blended to perfection." *New York Times* Bestselling Author Jayne Rylon

Carrie Ann Ryan's books are wickedly funny and deliciously hot, with plenty of twists to keep you guessing. They'll keep you up all night!" USA Today Bestselling Author Cari Quinn

"Once again, Carrie Ann Ryan knocks the Dante's Circle series out of the park. The queen of hot, sexy, enthralling paranormal romance, Carrie Ann is an author not to miss!" *New York Times* bestselling Author Marie Harte

Dedication

To the ones that found my wolves first.

Acknowledgments

The Talon Pack is near and dear to my heart and diving into my wolves and their magic always makes me remember why I write romance in the first place. Writing Mitchell and Dawn's story was almost bittersweet for me because it felt like a new series inside of two bigger worlds.

And because of that, I have a few people to thank. I couldn't do it without them.

To Chelle Olson, thank you for knowing my worlds as well as I do and helping me find my wolves. You're not only the best editor ever, you've become one of my closest friends. Love you honey.

To Charity, Tara, and Dr. Hubby, thank you for finishing out Team Carrie Ann and making sure each book is as cared for as the last—sometimes even more!

Thank you Kennedy Layne and Stacey Kennedy for pushing me five to seven days a week to finish this book. Without our coffee chats I don't think I'd be as sane as I am. And yes, girls, I heard that giggle, I'm perfectly okay. LOL

And to my readers...thank you again for being there for me.

Without you dear readers, I couldn't write the worlds I love. People keep telling me paranormal romance is dead but we know better, don't we?

Shifters forever!

Long Love the Pack!

~Carrie Ann

Destiny Disgraced

∞

The Talon Pack continues with a new twist to the Packs and a revelation no one was prepared for.
Mitchell Brentwood is aware that others think he's the harsh taskmaster Beta trying to keep his Pack alive, but they only see what he wants them to know. He'd once thought he had his path laid out before him, but when his future was violently ripped away, he vowed he'd never let anyone close again—especially not a young wolf from a traitorous Pack.

Dawn Levin may be younger than the war that destroyed her people, but she knows she must still pay for their sins. She's ready to find her way in this new world where wolves and humans blend as one, but first, she needs to fight her attraction to the dark wolf that stands in her way.

While the two struggle with their feelings and burning attraction for each other, they can't ignore the world that shakes beneath their feet. There is a new enemy on the horizon, one with revenge and the unknown on their minds. An adversary that might be closer than they realize.

CHAPTER ONE

D eath was but a whisper away, and yet Mitchell Brentwood couldn't breathe. With a slow blink, he moved to the side as a fist came at him, his opponent struggling to keep up with Mitchell's moves. As the youth was only a teenager and still learning while Mitchell was the Beta of the Talon Pack, he didn't blame the pup for not being fast enough.

He'd just train the kid until he sweated and cursed Mitchell out and *then* maybe the teen would be ready for whatever came next.

That was how Packs worked—always ready for the next battle, the next fight.

An odd thought for a wolf without a war to face.

He'd spent his life preparing for conflict or fighting an unseen master he'd never thought to find his way out from under, and now here he was, training young wolves to help them control their beasts, yet...alone.

His cousin Kameron punched his shoulder and frowned at him. Well, if one could call it a frown considering the man rarely if ever showed *any* emotion—no anger, no disappointment, no sadness, and certainly not a smile. While some called Mitchell a hard-ass bastard, they called Kameron the cold-ass one.

"What?" Mitchell growled. The punch hadn't hurt since Kameron hadn't put any heat behind it, but he still wasn't expecting it. And considering he and his brother, Max, had been raised with the rest of the cousins as if they were brothers, it was the principle of the thing.

"Your mind is wandering, and you're not paying attention." Kameron's gaze was on the juveniles in front of them and their training and not on him, so he flipped his cousin off. "Saw that. I'm pretty sure the kids saw that, too. Good job, oh fearless leader."

"Suck me," Mitchell whispered so low that only Kameron could hear. Since the trainees in front of them were also wolves, they had exceptional hearing, so he had to be careful how loud he spoke when he didn't want others to listen in.

"No, thanks, cousin. Why don't you find yourself a woman to do that? Maybe if you finally get laid, you'll wipe that perpetual scowl off your face."

A familiar ache pulsated deep inside, and it took everything within him not to let the pain cascading through him show on his face. He'd spent years perfecting that ability, yet each time it seemed to grow, increasing in need and dread.

Mitchell lashed out, kicking Kameron on the back of his knee. And though Mitchell was one of the best fighters in the Pack, he wasn't *the* best. That title belonged to their Enforcer—Kameron. While Mitchell was the Beta of the Talons and in charge of the day-to-day needs of the Pack, Kameron, as the Enforcer, was in charge of their defense. It only made sense that his cousin would be a slightly better fighter—it was genetic. So instead of his foot making contact, Kameron leapt out of the way so gracefully that he could have been a dancer in another life instead of a soldier.

Then, they fought.

Well, not really, as they weren't landing their punches or kicks, but they'd spent decades learning each other's moves and weaknesses. Even though neither of them was the Alpha or the strongest wolf in the Pack, they still fought like what they were—some of the best.

The younger wolves around them stopped what they were doing to watch the older wolves fight, and Mitchell didn't fault them for that. There was a reason he and his family were the highest in the hierarchy of the Pack, and they were damn good at what they did to protect their people. After a few minutes, they were both sweaty, their shirts sticking to their skin. Kameron's mouth twitched as if he were smiling. For his non-emotive cousin, that was big.

"Maybe you should think about your dick and get off mine," Mitchell said with a sneer.

"Why does everything you're saying today sound so dirty?" Kameron asked, wiping his face with the bottom of his shirt. A few sighs sounded from some of the women in their training group, and Mitchell held back a snort. There was always someone lusting after Kam, as if they wanted to be the one to melt his icy exterior.

Not too many panted after Mitchell, and he was just fine with that. He'd done his best to make his asshole persona permanent for a reason.

"You're just a pervert," Mitchell finally answered as he rolled his shoulders. "You can't help it, though, you're from *that* line of the Brentwoods."

Kameron flipped him off and almost smiled again. Two times in one day, that had to be a record. "Like your line is any better." He shook his head and turned to the others, watching them. "Okay, that's a wrap for the day. Let's cool down. Then you guys get to hear what your next assignment is."

Mitchell nodded. "You guys did good. All of you are learning to not only use your bodies as tools, but you're controlling your beasts more and more." The same could not be said for some of the older wolves in the Pack. That was why tomorrow's training sessions would be with some of the dominants, who were already on shifts around the den. Even though the Pack wasn't at war, that didn't mean they could slack off in their training.

It had been a year since the final battle with the rogue human factions that didn't know if they wanted to control the wolves or wipe them from existence. The Talons and their allies, the Redwoods, had lost many and endured countless other horrors that left horrific memories that would never fade. But in the end, a great sacrifice had saved them all. Mitchell still wasn't sure how he felt about the fact that he hadn't been strong enough to protect his people. It was the sacrifice of the others—the *pain* of others, including his brother, Max—that had won the war. Mitchell had only been there to fight.

But there wasn't a battle to be fought with claw and fang now. The humans came out on the good side in the end, and now they were in a time of peace. A calm where the wolves were no longer stuck within their wards inside the den, afraid to go out in public for fear that they'd be attacked by those anxious of what they didn't know or understand. Now, his people could go out and do what they'd done for hundreds of

4

years before the Unveiling, before the wolves were forced out into the open, revealing their secrets.

Almost all of his Packmates had jobs outside the den. Hell, most of them had lived on the outside before everything crumbled down around them. When they'd been at war, things were a little tight within the wards, but they'd made it work because there hadn't been another option. So, while many of the wolves had shifts within the den depending on their strengths, they also had jobs and lives outside the Pack's domain.

It was how it should have been all along, and his people were just now getting used to the fact that this was how it would be again. Only this time, many of them weren't hiding in plain sight. There wasn't a national register for the shifters, as Washington had nixed that idea after the asshole senator, McMaster, was killed, but there were still some non-government sanctioned websites out there that had lists of names and information on shifters. His cousin and Alpha, Gideon, growled daily about the mere existence of it, but there was nothing they could do about it. In this age of technology, even humans had all of that information since it was out in the public for anyone to see. The wolves could only control so much.

So, yes, Mitchell's people could go out and have jobs like they had in the past, but now they had to deal with the added pressure of being a wolf in human's clothing. At least, that's what others called them. Mitchell knew he was more than that. He was both—a wolf and a human, not just one or the other. That was how all shifters were, and they struggled with that balance every day. Hence the training sessions for juveniles and young adults like they just had. Adding hormones to the mix usually just made keeping control of one's wolf that much harder.

DESTINY DISGRACED

And yet, with all the talk of peace, Mitchell had a feeling there was something else coming. He'd spent most of his life either at war or fighting battles within his own Pack, yet he felt his sense of knowing wasn't because he *missed* the tension and anxiety. He just knew there was no way that things could suddenly be perfect and harmonious after everything that happened.

Something was going to change their peace, and Mitchell would be ready for it.

Not matter what it took.

"You headed over to Gideon's?" Kameron asked, rubbing the back of his neck. "I have to go help one of the soldiers with a problem on the outer perimeter, but Gideon said he wanted to see us at some point."

Mitchell nodded. "I planned to stop by." Plus, it would give him a chance to see his new niece. Though Gideon and the others weren't technically his brothers, making the newest additions to the Brentwoods second cousins or something like that, everyone had taken to calling Max and Mitchell uncles anyway.

Max didn't have a mate, and after the attack that had scarred his brother in more ways than one, Mitchell wasn't sure that Max *wanted* a mate. And as for Mitchell...well...he knew for a fact that he wouldn't find his mate. Ever.

There were just some things set in stone, and Mitchell being alone for the rest of his unnaturally long life was one of them.

"Let him and Brie know I'll stop by before dinner," Kameron said before lifting his chin and heading to wherever he needed to be.

Mitchell sighed and made his way over to Gideon's since he didn't have any other plans for a few hours. He figured he might as well see what his Alpha needed instead of sitting alone in his house, wondering what the hell to do. And, damn, he needed to stop sounding so depressing. It had been easier when he had battles and strategy to plan, or when the den was bursting at the seams with people. Since it was his job to ensure that every Pack member had a roof over their heads and was situated enough for their wolves to remain calm, he had plenty to do when everyone was forced within the den under their failing wards.

Now, the wards were rebuilt thanks to his cousin Brandon and his two mates, and people had started moving back into their homes outside the den. That meant there was less for Mitchell to do. And he hated it.

As he made his way to the front of Gideon's house, he heard the giggle of a sweet one-year-old and pushed all those thoughts to the side. Gideon and Brie's daughter, Fallon, toddled over to him, though she almost tripped a few times. He bent down to pick her up, brushing his lips over the top of her head when he pulled her close. She patted his mouth with her tiny hands and babbled incoherently. He was pretty sure a few of the things she said were actually words, but he couldn't make sense of them.

Only Gideon and Brie could understand their daughter, the same as how his cousin Ryder and his wife Leah could understand their son, Bryson Roland. In the past year, there'd been three new Brentwoods born into the world—well, two Brentwoods and a Jamenson since his cousin Brynn mated a Redwood wolf named Finn. They'd had their daughter Mackenzie a couple of months ago, around the same time that Bryson was born. Still, the fact that there was three more was a whole hell of a lot, considering there hadn't been an addition to their family in over a century. They were wolves after all, and lived ages longer than humans. They could spend lifetimes alone before eventually finding their mates, and some even waited longer to have children, preferring to spend time as a mated couple before adding to their family. The fact that the Brentwoods kept finding their mates in such quick succession would have worried Mitchell, but it wasn't as if he would find *his* mate. Not with everything he'd been through in the past.

"I see," Mitchell said solemnly, nodding his head as Fallon continued her conversation. He thought he heard something about a puppy, but that could have been any number of people in their wolf form, so he honestly didn't know.

"You're good with her," Brie, his Alpha's mate, said with a small smile. He hated the way she always seemed to see too much of him. She was a submissive wolf mated to the Alpha of their Pack. And while it might not make sense to outsiders, it made all the sense in the world to those inside the wards. She protected the Pack in her own way, her worth and contribution to the Pack's needs something none of them even knew they were missing until she showed up and took care of them.

If he weren't such a jerk, he might have been nicer to her, but he needed to keep her at a distance. He needed to keep *everyone* at arm's length.

"She's easy," he said with a shrug before handing Fallon over to her mother. "Gideon said he wanted to talk to me," he added instead of saying hello.

Brie ran her hand down Fallon's back as the little girl started to doze off. It must have been near her naptime, or the little girl wouldn't have started to fall asleep so easily. She was usually a burst of energy and babbles.

"He had to go meet with Kade, but he told me he texted you." She rocked back and forth as Fallon fell fully asleep in her mother's arms. The little girl would one day be Alpha—a first for the Talons, and maybe even all the Packs as Mitchell hadn't heard of a female Alpha before. It wasn't that they weren't strong or capable because, hell, female dominants were tougher than most men he knew. No, it was because becoming the Alpha, Heir, Beta, Enforcer, Omega, or Healer wasn't something someone could fight for or try to attain. Those titles were bestowed—he held back a mental cringe at that word—upon them by the moon goddess. The goddess had made the first wolf, the first shifter, and also determined the hierarchies needed for a Pack. Mitchell hadn't learned until recently that those first goddess-touched were Talons. In fact, the first wolves who made the Pack were actually *reincarnated* as the triplets—Kameron, Walker, and Brandon.

Mitchell still wasn't sure he quite believed that and, hell, didn't know if he *wanted* to, but it wasn't his business, so he chose not to think about it.

"Mitchell?"

He shook himself out of those thoughts and held back a curse as he pulled out his phone and saw that he had indeed missed a text from Gideon. "I didn't feel it vibrate and didn't have the ringer on since we were training. Sorry to bother you at naptime."

Brie just smiled and shook her head. "You're never a bother. Do you want to come in for something to drink? I'm headed to the maternal council meeting in a bit, but I have an hour or so."

Mitchell was shaking his head before she'd finished her sentence. He preferred being alone to having Brie so close where she saw too much of him.

And it always hurt him when he remembered exactly who she reminded him of.

He quickly pushed those thoughts from his brain and did his best not to rub at the three jagged scars on his chest. He'd been too in his head today and needed to do something different, or he'd end up drowning himself in a bottle of tequila later and be of no use to anyone.

"I need to pick up a few things from town. I should get on that. Do you need anything?" The den was pretty self-sufficient and had enough land to remain that way for years, but they'd been trying to do more outside the den walls since the end of the war. Mitchell was only doing his part, he reminded himself. He wasn't running away. Not again.

"Can you pick up a bag of coffee beans from that shop down on First?" she asked with a bright smile. "I know I can get beans in bulk online or even at another store, but now that I'm allowed caffeine again, I seemed to have found myself a new craving. If it's out of your way, though, I can pick some up later."

Mitchell nodded even as he went through his memory to see if he'd ever actually been inside that shop. He knew that Brynn loved that place and still went there with her mate, but he didn't venture into coffee shops much. Too many people, and way too many scents for his wolf nose.

"Just tell me what kind you want and how much, and I'll pick them up." He made a note in his phone when she told him the name then gave her a nod and walked away.

His wolf had begun prowling inside him, and he wasn't sure if it was about Brie or what she represented. Either way, he needed to get far enough away that he could calm his wolf and forget about the pain that he lived with every day.

10

Because the one thing they didn't talk about when it came to mating was that if a bond broke, a wolf could still feel it. Mitchell felt the echo of what had been, the life he'd been promised, with every breath.

But he'd lost all that, and had learned to live like he was now.

His mate was dead.

And wolves like him didn't get second chances.

Ever.

CHAPTER TWO

awn Levin's feet hurt, and her hair smelled of coffee and, for some reason, hazelnut, but since that meant she had a job and therefore a paycheck, she didn't care. Her wolf stretched her legs before curling up for a nap inside her, and Dawn held back a smile. She'd gone running late last night under the crescent moon since she wasn't able to sleep, and her wolf had wanted to play. So now, at least one of them was partially satisfied for the time being.

The human part of her, well...at least she had a job and a relatively stable roof over her head once she went back to the den.

She filled another order, pulling two shots of espresso as she frowned. Was her home *technically* called a den? She wasn't sure, but her family had always called it that since they didn't have another word for it.

She was a Central Pack wolf. A wolf who *technically* didn't have a Pack at all since the Centrals weren't yet recognized by the moon goddess or many of the other Packs in the country. Before she was born, the former Alpha and many of his followers had done horrible things and ended up killing most of the Pack in the process.

Dawn had been taught the violent history at a young age like the rest of the children she'd grown up with. The elders hadn't wanted there to be secrets. They'd also wanted any hotheads within the Pack to learn from past mistakes.

"Dawn, hurry up. We're running behind."

She winced at her boss's words and went back to making foam. She could usually do most of her work in her sleep, but with her brain going in a thousand different directions today, she apparently couldn't quite keep up.

The door opened and she looked to see her friend and fellow wolf, Sam, walk through holding his empty canvas bag. He was their delivery boy and jack-of-all-trades. She liked the fact that she had a Pack member who ventured out of the den every so often, but she knew she still did more than others. Sam was learning to be more human these days since her Pack had hidden themselves even more after the Unveiling, but now she had a friend she got to see every day outside the den, as well.

"Hey," he said with a wink. "Got anything for me?"

She nodded and gestured toward the end of the coffee bar. Since her boss was still watching, she didn't talk to Sam before he headed out, but she knew she'd see him back at the den. He was older, and their wolves far different, but they fit together nicely on the fringes of a Pack that wasn't a Pack.

"Vanilla latte with two pumps of vanilla," she called out, pulling herself from her thoughts, and set the drink on the counter before going back to the long line of cups waiting for her. She needed to keep her head on her work and not on a past she couldn't change.

Only it was never that easy since she lived with reminders of that past every day. Her people were on the verge of becoming a true Pack, recognized by the other Packs and the moon goddess. No one knew *why* they knew, but there was a knowing in the air, and the other Alphas around them apparently knew it, too. She wasn't sure what it all meant except for the fact that things would change soon. Dawn just hoped it would all be for the best.

Her Pack didn't have an Alpha or a Healer, or anyone that could truly help their people in times of need. That meant there hadn't been any matings since her parents mated before the Centrals fell. And without matings, there were no more babies or growth.

Therefore, a maternal dominant like Dawn had no purpose other than to smile and make coffee and hope that any income she had would be enough for their meager coffers.

And that was enough of that. She went back to focusing on the coffee orders. She was just finishing up the last of the rush when the hairs on the back of her neck stood on end. Her wolf perked up, causing a mix of fear and anticipation to slide over her skin.

Him.

She knew it was him.

Only one person in the world made her feel this way.

Someone she'd never truly spoken to.

Mitchell Brentwood. Beta of the Talon Pack.

And pain in her ass.

Why this wolf was in her coffee shop, she didn't know. She'd been working as a barista for a few years now and had seen many of the Talon Pack members walk through the door, yet Mitchell wasn't one of them. The only reason she even knew who he was came from the fact that he visited her den often these days. He met with her brother at least once a week and had been there when the wards fell that fateful day. But he'd never spoken to her.

And for some reason, that pissed off her wolf to no end.

He was too damn sexy for his own good, as well. All dark and handsome with hair a deep shade of brown, light brown skin that didn't look as if it came from the sun but from genetics, and even darker eyes that bored holes into her.

Her wolf scratched at her, either wanting out or wanting to growl at the man waiting in line, but Dawn did what she did best and ignored it. She had a job to do and bills to pay. Thinking about why a wolf annoyed her wouldn't help any of that.

Of course, as soon as she thought that, Mitchell met her gaze and raised a brow. Yes, she was a Central wolf working as a barista at a coffee shop downtown. It wasn't as glamorous as some of the other jobs wolves had, but she only had a home-schooled high school education, and that wasn't enough for some places.

So, instead of focusing on why this wolf set her on edge, she went back to making drinks, only to stop again when the familiar scents of her best friends walked through the door behind Mitchell.

Aimee, Dhani, and Cheyenne were human and some of the best women she knew. She'd met each of them over the past seven years working outside the den. And while she felt she could tell them almost anything, they didn't know she was a wolf. At first, it was because nobody knew about the wolves, and then, after the Unveiling, well... she'd been afraid to tell them who she truly was.

But everyone knew Mitchell Brentwood was a shifter. He'd been on the front lines during the battles and was televised all around the world. And while they may know his title, nobody knew exactly what the position entailed. The Talons and Redwoods had done their best to keep as many of their secrets and traditions as close to the vest as possible. Information like that in the wrong hands could spell catastrophe. The evidence of that was in the Unveiling itself, after all.

Once again, she shook off those thoughts and smiled at her friends, ignoring the way Mitchell followed her gaze. She really hoped that Mitchell wouldn't take the opportunity to speak to her for the first time. She didn't want to have to answer the hard questions from her friends about how she knew him.

While Cheyenne and Dhani went to grab their usual table, Aimee came over to the counter where Dawn was working and smiled. Of her friends, Aimee was the sweetest. While the others could be sweet, they also had an edge to them that Dawn and Aimee lacked. She figured that's why they all meshed so well; they each brought something different to their friendship and always looked out for one another.

Of course, Dawn would probably be a better friend at the end of the day if she actually told them who she truly was, but she couldn't. While she *knew* that none of them were bigots, she was still worried about how they would feel about her once they knew the truth. She'd hidden for so long, she didn't know how to open up. What made it worse was that if and when she actually told her friends about her other nature, she'd have to explain to them about her Pack's past. She wasn't part of a true Pack like the famous

Talons and Redwoods. And she wasn't even a lone wolf like some others out there. Her Pack was somewhere in between, with a legacy shamed by disgrace. And even though she hadn't been born when everything occurred, she still carried that shadow.

"Hey, you," Aimee said as she pulled up in front of Dawn. "We called in our order ahead of time since we knew you'd be busy."

Dawn looked down at the drinks in her hand and smiled back at her friend. "Working on them now, actually. I didn't look at the names since I was in the zone." Or at least she should have been. "I'll have your drinks ready in a minute if you want to wait here and keep me company."

"No problem." Aimee leaned over the counter and let out a small sigh.

Dawn knew that sigh, it meant that Aimee was feeling a lot more tired than she let on, but Dawn couldn't say anything about it. Not when Aimee got all secretive and pasted a smile on her face whenever Dawn mentioned it. And despite all of Dawn's enhanced senses, she couldn't figure out if Aimee's exhaustion came from working too hard at the diner or if there was something else going on.

"I'd take a break with you guys, but we're in the middle of our rush," she said, changing the subject while pulling two more shots of espresso. She sucked in a breath as Mitchell made his way to the front of the line and ordered coffee beans rather than a drink. She didn't know why she was suddenly disappointed that she wouldn't be making him anything, and she silently cursed herself for even thinking that.

"Is that Mitchell Brentwood?" Aimee asked, her voice low. But it wasn't low enough, not for a wolf. Because Mitchell turned sharply at Aimee's question and frowned at Dawn. "Crap," Aimee muttered, her face going beet red.

"Looks like it," Dawn said with a false sense of cheer. "Nice to see you, Mr. Brentwood," she added, trying to get his attention off her friend so she wouldn't be so embarrassed. Why she called him by his last name like that and not his first, she didn't know. Apparently, that's just what she decided to do in the rush of things.

"Dawn," Mitchell growled low with a nod of his head. He nodded at Aimee before taking his bag of beans and walking out of the shop.

"What. Was. That?" Aimee asked, her voice low. "He knew your name!"

Dawn swallowed hard, annoyed with herself for the tingles going up and down her spine at the sound of her name on his lips. Just because he was a *very* sexy shifter and her wolf seemed to be confused around him didn't mean she had to act like a wayward teenage pup and swoon over the man.

"I have a nametag," Dawn said, hoping her voice didn't sound as squeaky to Aimee as it did to her.

Aimee raised a brow. "Okay."

Dawn cleared her throat. "Anyway, here are your drinks. Tell the girls I said hi and that I'll be by for movie night tomorrow. Promise." She'd skipped the last two get-togethers because of Pack issues, and had missed a lot more things right after the Unveiling, so she'd promised herself she would do her best to be a better friend.

Even if that meant telling the girls everything.

Goddess, she hadn't lost them, but she knew she was losing more of herself every day that she kept the secret.

"Sounds like a plan," Aimee said sweetly. Dawn knew Aimee would tell the others about Mitchell's sudden need to speak to Dawn for the first time as soon as she got back to the table.

Dawn had a feeling things were going to get complicated. She just hoped she'd be strong enough to keep up.

A couple of hours later, when her shift was over, she texted her family that she was okay and headed to her second job at the daycare center. Even though the wars were over and wolves were supposed to be safe out in public, there were always fanatics. The number of hate crimes against wolves and witches was down from where it had been at the peak of the Unveiling, but they hadn't been eradicated completely. People feared what they didn't know, and were scared of anything different even more. So she texted her family every time she left one place for another just so they knew she was okay. She couldn't do much for them considering the strength of her wolf and her talents, but she could at least alleviate some of their worries.

Sometimes, it was difficult being the youngest member of the Centrals—or what was left of the Centrals. Children only came from mated pairs or triads. When the elders and some of the other wolves left the Central den all those years ago to hide from their Alpha's wrath, they hadn't been able to take many people with them. Anyone left bonded to the Pack within the den died because of the Alpha's actions. Those left were forced to stay where they were, hidden in the forest without a true Pack. And because her Pack couldn't form mating bonds anymore, there were no new couples to create children. Yes, some of the other mated pairs could have children well into their hundreds of years, but no one else after her parents had been blessed with a child. She honestly wasn't sure if it had been on purpose or not, and was too scared to even ask.

It just made things worse for her wolf. Wolves were either dominant or submissive—with varying degrees within each subset. She was neither. She was a maternal dominant. That meant her wolf's true calling was to be a protector of children. Her wolf needed to nurture and care for the young of the Pack. Yet without any pups within the den walls, a part of her always felt broken. Her wolf yearned to find its place among her people, to fulfill its duty, but the way things were going, her wolf may never find its destiny.

Hence why she volunteered at the local daycare. She didn't have the certification to be a full-time member and caretaker, but she could at least be around human babies enough to satisfy her wolf's desire to take care of pups. It wasn't ideal, and she knew her wolf wasn't completely happy, but it was the best she could do under the circumstances. Maybe when the moon goddess finally blessed them, she'd find her place.

Maybe then, she'd be more than a sad wolf with no true calling.

At that thought, a shiver washed over her, and she looked over her shoulder, feeling as though someone was watching her. The hairs on the back of her neck rose again, only this time, it wasn't because of the odd anticipation she felt when she saw Mitchell.

No, this was something different. Something was coming, but she had no idea what. Just as quickly as the feeling washed over her, it faded away, leaving her alone and confused. She shook it off and increased her pace as she made her way to the daycare center. She'd spend an hour there at most and then head back home. There was no use being careless and spending too much time out on the streets alone, especially when she felt as though someone may be watching her.

Her Pack was on the verge of change, and she knew not everyone was happy with that. No one knew who would become Alpha or goddess-blessed, though the Pack had a feeling it would be her brother. As for Dawn, no one thought much of anything about her. She was just who she was.

"You're being an idiot," she mumbled to herself. Annoyed, she quickly called the daycare center and told them she wouldn't be able to volunteer today. When her wolf was on edge like this, she knew better than to ignore the signs.

She needed her family and the relative safety of her den. With her wolf closer to the surface now, she headed to her car and drove the short distance to her den. There was one major city near the three shifter dens—the Redwoods, Talons, and Centrals—with a few smaller towns dotted around, as well. She knew of one other Pack, the Aspens, that lived a few hours south, but as far as she knew, she'd never met them. Thankfully, most of the area around where she lived was either owned outright by the other major wolf Packs, or it was considered a nature preserve.

She drove through the wards that surrounded her den and parked next to the small house where her family lived. The Centrals had been in hiding for so long that they hadn't built up their den like others had. So, she still lived in the home she'd grown up in with her parents and her brother, Cole—most likely their future Alpha.

As soon as she got out of her car, her brother walked out, a frown on his face and his arms open. They were close in age—both in their mid-twenties—and had grown up with only each other to lean on.

While she might not understand the path her brother was on now, she knew he'd always be there for her.

She leaned into him, inhaling the scent of his wolf that spoke of power and strength. Her wolf calmed. Dawn hadn't needed to say a word, yet he'd been there for her. That was Pack. That was family.

And maybe one day soon, the bonds that she'd only heard about that slid through wolves and anchored them to the moon goddess and each other would wind through her, as well.

But for now, she had her family. That was all she needed.

And no matter what, she wouldn't think about the scowling wolf who'd spoken directly to her for the first time that day. He didn't fit into her plans—no matter how much he intrigued her wolf.

CHAPTER THREE

B lood spilled to the ground, covering Mitchell's hands and knees as he bent over her prone body and tried not to move her. She was so fragile, so human, and covered in so much blood. Too much blood.

"Heather," he whispered, his voice cracking. "Don't move, baby."

She blinked her deep green eyes up at him and shivered, her gaze not quite right. He was losing her inch-by-inch, moment-by-moment, and there was nothing he could do.

Nothing she'd let him do.

"You did this," she whispered, her voice a rasp. "It was you. It's your fault."

He reared back, the darkness surrounding them growing ever closer. This wasn't right. This wasn't how it had happened. He stared at the blood on his hands, his body shaking.

He hadn't done this. He hadn't killed her.

But there was blood on his hands.

Mitchell sat up in bed, his sweat-slick skin sticking to his sheets. He peeled the top sheet off and grimaced before running his hand over his face. He hadn't had that dream in a few months, but it was just as vivid as ever. It always started the same—the blood, his fear, and the ragdoll look of Heather near him. But the ending changed every once in a while to either show him what had truly happened or manifest as his fear lashing out at him. At least in this version, she hadn't crawled to him like in one of those horror movies. That one hadn't let him sleep soundly again for almost a month.

He'd lost Heather decades ago, yet he still dreamed of her.

That's what happened when you lost half of your soul—you didn't get it back.

"Goddess, help me," he muttered, not really expecting an answer. She may have spoken to some of his cousins, but she'd never shown herself to him. If it weren't for the fact that he could literally shift into a wolf when he wanted to and feel the Pack bonds as well as the tie that spoke to him as Beta, he'd have thought the goddess just a figment of someone's imagination.

Annoyed that he'd woken up like he had and would never be able to get back to sleep, he got out of bed and stripped it before heading to the laundry room. He tossed the sheets and his sweaty shorts in and started the load. He had other laundry to do, but he wanted to get rid of the evidence of his sleepless night.

Though he wanted coffee, he figured a shower would probably be the best idea. He could still feel and scent the sweat on his skin, and he wouldn't be able to get comfortable until he washed it off. It wasn't quite sunrise yet, and that meant he had a few hours until he met up with his brother and headed to the meeting with the Packs. He could at least get a few things done around the house since he was up at this ungodly hour.

Mitchell walked naked into his bathroom and into the shower stall, turning on the water to full blast before it heated up. His wolf growled deep inside at the rush of cold over their skin, but he ignored it. After sweating through his sheets like he had, the frigid temperature was a blessing. He quickly washed his hair and body, his eyes not quite open since he hadn't slept well.

As he slowly woke up, so did another part of him, and since he only got relief from his hands these days, he gripped himself, squeezing the base slightly. Water slid down his back, and he added soap to his hand so he could glide over himself with ease; his fist clenching around his length as vivid images of soft blond hair and blue eyes filled his mind.

He paused for only a second, his brain misfiring since that image wasn't one he normally thought of when he made himself come. Annoyed, yet still in need of release, he pushed thoughts of that particular woman away and tried to get his orgasm over with. Of course, his mind and wolf never seemed to listen to him these days, so now he couldn't help but picture Dawn licking her lips.

With a growl, he picked up his pace and pumped his hips, visions of Dawn on her knees as she took him into her mouth, and then him making her come over and over again filling his mind. When his balls tightened, he fisted his other hand against the shower wall and came hard, his body shaking, and thoughts of Dawn never leaving his mind.

Cursing, he cleaned himself up again and turned off the now cooling water. What the hell had that been about? He'd *never* thought of anyone but Heather when he came. Hell, these past few years, he'd only thought about the shadow of a woman since it'd been so long since he held Heather in his arms. Now, with just one spoken word to the woman he'd been avoiding for the past year, he'd jacked off to her?

Bile filled his mouth, and he bent over the sink, trying to calm himself so he didn't throw up. His soul belonged to another—even if she hadn't fully understood what that meant at the time. He didn't have the right to think of anyone else like that, let alone a younger wolf who hadn't yet seen the world, and especially a woman he didn't even know. She might be beautiful and may even have a spine of steel considering what Pack she'd grown up in, but she wasn't for him.

No one was anymore.

Disgusted with himself, he wiped his face and brushed his teeth before pulling on the clothes he'd laid out. He had to see his brother before he went to the all-Packs meeting later that day. Honestly, he wasn't in the mood to do either, but he didn't really have a choice.

Max hadn't been the same since the final attack on the den that left so many of them dead or injured. Once, Max had been the smiling one of the Brentwoods, the only one who seemed to have made it out of the prior dictatorship within the Talon Pack emotionally whole. That couldn't be said anymore, and Mitchell hated the loss, but letting Max know that wouldn't help anything.

Pushing thoughts of that and whatever the hell he'd been thinking about in the shower firmly out of his mind, he headed over to Max's home that wasn't that far from Mitchell's. All of the current Brentwoods lived within the den walls, though now it was by choice and not how it had been before Mitchell became the Beta. His uncle, the former Alpha and his cousins' father, had been an asshole to the highest degree and hadn't wanted anyone in his family to have a life of their own. So though some, like Mitchell himself, had been forced to have jobs outside the den to put money in the family's coffers, they'd been forced to live under the archaic rule of an Alpha who didn't care for his people.

Things were different now, but sometimes it was hard to throw away decades of memories and learn to live in the now. Shaking his head, he knocked on Max's door before walking right in since he'd never needed an invitation in the past to see his sibling. And if Max had a problem with that, well, Mitchell would just force his little brother to deal with it. Treating Max as anything but who he'd always been would only hurt him in the long run—at least that's what Mitchell figured. He could be doing all of this wrong and might end up making things worse, but he was at a loss for what to do. Normally open-and-honest Max was now closed off tighter than a drum. None of the others in the Pack—Mitchell included—could get to his little brother through Pack bonds. Max had bottled up his emotions and needs so tightly that no one could help.

Not that they'd know what to do if they could...

"Max, you ready to go?" Mitchell called out.

Silence greeted him, and he let out a sigh before going into the living room and starting to clean up. It wasn't that his brother was messy, it was as if Max just didn't care anymore. Clothes were strewn about, and books were left open and stacked on top of one another. There wasn't any dust or garbage around, but things were a little cluttered—something that had never been the case before the attack.

"You don't need to clean up after me," Max said softly from the doorway.

Mitchell looked up sharply, though he'd scented his brother before the other man spoke. "I don't mind."

Max snorted. "Yeah, you do. It's fine, Mitchell. You don't have to act like the nice one."

Mitchell just shook his head and piled up the clothing in different hampers Max had left out in the living room. "Shut up. I'm just helping since I'm here and I don't like messes."

"Helping because you want to? Or because you think I can't do it myself?" Max growled and held up what was left of his right arm. The explosion that had taken out part of the den had also taken his brother's arm below the elbow. Shifters could heal many things, but they couldn't regrow limbs or organs.

Mitchell let out a sigh, and the scars on his brother's face and neck tightened. Since Max wore a long-sleeved shirt—with one arm pinned up—Mitchell couldn't see the rest of the jagged scars that ran along his chest and body, but he knew they were there. He'd watched his cousin Walker, their Healer, try his best to piece Max back together after the maniac who'd attacked them took out his personal wrath on Max, but it hadn't been enough. There had been such trauma to Max's body that his brother hadn't been able to heal without scarring. Maybe, one day, his body would heal more, but for now, every time Mitchell's brother looked in a mirror or down at himself, he would see the evidence of what happened.

No wonder Max didn't laugh anymore.

"We need to head to the all-Packs meeting. Gideon wants us both there." Mitchell was going in his role as Beta since all the Packs needed their Alphas and Betas there. In addition to the lieutenants who would be there for the Alphas' safety as their security force, each Pack could also bring one additional member. Gideon wanted Max since he was not only a council member, but also a calming force. Usually. Mitchell wasn't sure the latter was true anymore, but if Gideon wanted it done, they did it.

Max met his eyes for a brief moment, the gold rim around the irises telling him that Max's wolf was close to the surface.

"Don't know why he needs me there. There are other council members that could go."

"Because he wants you!" Mitchell yelled, then cursed inwardly when Max flinched. "Shit. I'm sorry. I had a crappy night, and I shouldn't take it out on you. But, seriously, Gideon wants one of the council members with him since I think Kade is bringing one of the Redwood members that you work with. This should be an easy enough meeting, but you know how Blade is." Blade was the Alpha of the Aspens and an asshole on most days.

Max ran his hand over his face and let out a breath. "I need to find my shoes." He turned but halted before he made his way back to his bedroom. "Nightmares again?"

Mitchell swallowed hard. "Yeah."

"You ever going to tell us why you have them? Or what happened that night?"

"Get moving, Max," Mitchell growled softly instead of answering. "We don't want to be late and give Blade any ammunition."

Max didn't say anything, but Mitchell saw his brother's shoulders drop. However much Mitchell wanted to have Max whole and healthy again, he knew that there were some things he couldn't tell. Some secrets were better left buried.

Gideon pinched the bridge of his nose, and Mitchell had a feeling his Alpha was about to reach across the table and throttle Blade. Frankly, it was just another day at an all-Packs meeting.

The name of the meeting was actually a misnomer since it was only the three Packs of the Pacific Northwest that met up like this. Mitchell wasn't sure there had ever been a true all-Packs meeting, and he didn't think there ever would be. Too many dominant wolves in one place meant that things could go haywire, quickly. Parker, their new Pack member, was the Voice of the Wolves and had met each Alpha over time to try and pave the way for connections, but Mitchell knew that, in some cases, that might be a lost cause.

Their animals were far too close to the surface to truly come together.

However, Gideon and Kade were trying to bring at least some semblance of peace to their territories. The war that had taken out the Centrals over thirty years ago came about because of greed and lack of communication. No one wanted that to happen again, so the Redwoods and Talons were trying to make sure they met and were kept in the loop on some things.

The Aspens, however, never looked like they wanted to be there.

"I'm just saying," Blade drawled, "I don't think the Centrals have a right to be a Pack. They called a *demon* to our world. Who knows what would have happened if we hadn't taken it out."

"We?" Kade asked, his head tilting like that of his wolf. "I don't remember you coming to our aid when my parents died on the battlefield, and my son was left to become the Heir when he could barely shift." Nick, Kade's other son and Beta to the Redwoods, leaned forward, but not in aggression. Mitchell figured the kid—who wasn't really a kid anymore—was just trying to keep his father's temper under control.

Blade narrowed his eyes, but before he could say anything else, his Beta, a woman named Audrey, tapped her knuckles on the table.

"This isn't getting us anywhere," she said calmly.

Mitchell studied the woman and tried to figure her out. While her Alpha was a royal bastard, Audrey seemed like she had a decent head on her shoulders. She was the first female Beta he'd ever met, but in all honesty, he hadn't met that many since he spent so much of his life under lock and key. There was something...off about her, though, and he couldn't quite place it.

She must have felt his gaze because she turned to glare at him, and he gave her a nod, trying to ease the tension.

"We don't have a say in whether the Centrals become a Pack or not," Mitchell said after a moment.

"The hell we don't," Blade spat, and Mitchell could have sworn Audrey sighed.

"We don't choose which groups become a Pack," Gideon said softly, his voice firm. "That is up to the moon goddess. We might not be old enough to remember how it is when a Pack is first birthed, but we all know the stories. The signs. The Centrals paid a penance that was never theirs to pay."

"Bullshit," the Aspen lieutenant hissed. Mitchell didn't know the other man's name, but he always sided with Blade.

"Those who attacked the Redwoods are long dead," Kade said over the other man's curses. "If anyone should have an issue with the Centrals getting the blessing from the moon goddess, it's my Pack, but we are *all* in agreement that those left to become a new Pack don't deserve our wrath."

Mitchell nodded. "They were the ones who left when they could, knowing they could die because of the Pack bonds, but they did so for their children. They've spent thirty years living a shadow of a life because they never felt like they would be welcome anywhere—and hell, I'm not sure they were wrong about that, at least at some points in these past years with everyone going on—but their wolves *need* that connection. Not everyone can go lone wolf."

"Not everyone should have to," Max said softly, surprising Mitchell. Max had been silent up until then, as if trying to keep the others from noticing him. Now, those who didn't know Max stared at his scars, and Mitchell wanted to run his claws over anyone who dared to look at his brother in any way other than seeing the sacrifices Max had made for his Pack.

"We're not here to decide if the Centrals deserve power," Gideon said after a moment. "We all know this Cole will be Alpha. Our wolves know it, and our elders have spoken. But what we *can* do is help him. He's never lived under an Alpha. He and his sister were born *after* they left the Centrals. They need guidance."

"Do you think his sister could be goddess-blessed, as well?" Audrey asked curiously.

Mitchell stiffened at the mention of Dawn but tried to downplay it. "We won't know until it happens. Only the Alpha seems to be showing up right now."

"Odd," Audrey said. "However, it's not like we've ever witnessed something like this before."

"Exactly," Gideon said. "This means we can't stand back and let them falter. While I trust this Cole to a certain extent, if they are left to fend for themselves and fail, it could lead to something far worse."

"So you're saying you want to control them?" Blade asked.

The other two Alphas shook their heads in unison. "No," Kade answered. "We want to let them know they aren't alone."

"Being alone led to war and the Unveiling," Gideon said softly.

"Many things led to the Unveiling," Mitchell put in. It wasn't the Talons' fault for what happened, even though they had been the ones to first appear in public. With the way technology was, it was bound to happen eventually.

But from the look on Blade's face, the other man didn't agree.

"We'll help," Audrey put in quickly.

Blade glared at her, and Mitchell knew there was something else going on, something that he couldn't place. His own wolf was on edge, and he didn't know why. Blade rubbed him the wrong way, and he would have to mention to Kameron that they needed to keep an eye on this Alpha.

Because with everyone's attention on the Centrals and making sure their peace with the humans stayed civil, Mitchell had a feeling they were missing something even bigger. And an oversight like that could be deadly.

CHANGE

Blade wasn't a fan of change. He'd spent the past century watching the humans as they created one thing after another, becoming more and more in tune with technology and forgetting the environment that sustained everything around them. Not that Blade considered himself an environmentalist, but when his people lived in the woods, hidden under magical wards, he tended to care if a tree was around or not to hide what he needed concealing.

His Pack was more insular than most, and that was for a good reason. The Redwoods and Talons thought they had more secrets, but they didn't know the Aspens. Blade had been Alpha long enough to know that in order to *ensure* the secrets he wanted buried were kept, change had to come when *he* wanted it.

Not when the damned Talons decided.

He'd had enough of listening to those two upstart Alphas who weren't even born when he became Alpha telling him what to do. He'd listened to their damn *representative*, Parker, for as long as he could manage before he practically threw the over-confident pup out of his wards.

The Talons might think they were the ones responsible for the new strengthened wards and the fact that the humans were no longer looking to war with his people, but Blade wasn't so sure about that. He didn't have proof. All he had were bragging pups who thought they knew better than he did.

And now, they wanted to allow the Centrals back into the mix? The Aspens weren't so sure about that.

He'd never hungered for more power than he currently had, but maybe it was time to step out and set the others straight. They'd been the ones to begin this change. Now, Blade would be the one to end it.

One way or another.

CHAPTER FOUR

"I'm sorry. I know I'm a flake these days, but my family needs me." Dawn sighed into the phone, but Aimee didn't sigh back.

Thankfully. Dawn paced her small living room, worried she was messing everything up. She'd called Aimee instead of Dhani or Cheyenne because while she might be a strong wolf, she was a wuss when it came to backing out of plans with her best friends. Though she'd told herself she wouldn't back out of this one, she hadn't had a choice when Cole came to her with dinner plans over at the Talon den.

One didn't say no to the Talons when they invited you over for dinner as a peace offering. Sam had already been by to make sure she was okay and ready to go, but she wasn't a hundred percent calm.

"I totally understand," Aimee said softly. Her friend coughed, and Dawn frowned. Aimee had apparently caught another cold—her fourth of this year already. Dawn knew humans were far more fragile than wolves, but Aimee seemed more delicate than most. "Family comes first," her friend continued.

CARRIE ANN RYAN

Family. Pack. They always came first...though she couldn't say that. Dawn hated keeping secrets and knew that once the Centrals became a Pack in truth, she'd have to tell her friends everything.

"Thanks for understanding. I want to promise that I'll be at the next one, too..."

"But you hate lying," Aimee finished for her. "I get it, and Dhani and Cheyenne will too. It's not like we all don't have other responsibilities outside of watching a movie together when we can."

"Yeah, but mine have been taking up more time lately."

"True, but we love you anyway. Now, get what you need to do, done. We'll miss you."

"I'll miss you, too." She and Aimee talked for a few more minutes before letting each other go. If it weren't for the fact that this was the first time the Alpha couple of the Talons had invited her family over, Dawn might have made her excuses, but this was a big deal for her den.

It was just one step closer to them being recognized as a true Pack. They needed the moon goddess's touch, of course, but without the local wolves' acknowledgment and treaties, her small, pretty much defenseless Pack wouldn't last too long.

They were wolves, after all, not humans. Only the strong survived, no matter how civilized they pretended to be.

"You ready to go? Mom and Dad are going to stay here since we need soldiers in the den and they're still the strongest wolves we have other than us."

Dawn turned at her brother's words and nodded. When her small faction of the Centrals had left the old Pack years ago, her parents were the youngest pair. Most of the wolves in the prior den hadn't been able to sever ties since their Alpha's word was law and

37

betraying that bond was physically impossible for some. Somehow, her parents had found the strength to leave with the elders who were able to hide away with some of the children, but it had almost killed them in the process.

"So, it's just the two of us?" she asked, wiping her hands down her pants. She'd gone with black pants and a billowy top so she'd be able to move quickly if needed, but something that still looked decent enough for a dinner with such high-ranking wolves.

Now, she was just being silly. These were normal people. Sure, they were all much stronger and put-together than she or her brother, but they wouldn't eat them and pick their teeth with their bones like some of the old stories of her former Pack. Right?

"Yep." Cole grinned at her, and she couldn't help but smile back. Her brother looked like her, but with a slightly darker shade of blond hair. He had the same eyes and smile when he dared to show the softer side of himself. His wolf was far more dominant than hers, however, and she was just fine with that. Her wolf *needed* a dominant around. That's how shifter Packs worked. She knew her brother had to be scared to death of becoming the true leader and Alpha of her small Pack, but she also knew he had the capability to be great at it. He cared for everyone in his sights and did his best to soak up any knowledge he could. He, like she, was only in his twenties, however, and had never lived under an Alpha's rule. She could only hope that working with Gideon and Mitchell like he was would help him gain confidence in what he was doing. She knew he was also talking with the Redwood Heir and Beta, but she hadn't been part of those meetings. The fact that it was the Redwoods who the Centrals attacked made things a little tricky in her opinion, but the Redwoods seemed to have forgiven those Centrals who were left.

It was all just so confusing, and some days, she just wanted to be a barista instead of the wolf she was.

Cole's hand went to the back of her neck, and he frowned down at her. She leaned into his touch, her wolf curling into a comfortable ball at the feeling of her brother's wolf. They were Pack creatures without a Pack, and sometimes, the effects of the lack of bond were greater than others.

"What's wrong, Dawny?"

She scrunched her face at the nickname. "I'm just nervous since it's our first dinner like this. And could you not call me Dawny in front of the entire Talon Pack? I'm going as your second here, and that name doesn't really invoke strength and stability."

He rolled his eyes even as his smile widened. Well, at least she'd gotten him to smile again since he didn't do much of that lately. "I'll do my best. And, Dawn? Try not to be too nervous, okay? I know this is a big deal tonight, but we need to act casual."

She met his eyes, and they both broke out into laughter. "Yeah, casual isn't happening." Especially not if Mitchell was around tonight, but that wasn't something she was prepared to talk to her brother about just then. Or ever.

"Well, as long as we don't ignite a war, we should end up ahead."

Dawn winced. "Yeah, let's not do that. That means no insulting the food."

Cole stepped back and placed his hand over his heart. "Cruel woman. I *never* insult food...unless it's yours."

"Brat." She punched him in the side, and he mock shuddered since she knew there was no way her slight hit even registered to him. Her brother was damn strong and only getting stronger.

"You're younger than I am, you know. You're the brat. *I'm* the big brother."

"Whatever you say. Now, come on, Alpha-to-be, let's show the Talons we Centrals aren't heathens."

He sighed and took her hand as they made their way out of their house and toward Cole's truck. "Don't call me Alpha yet, okay? I know everyone knows it and is thinking it, but I don't want to have the title said aloud around me until I've earned it."

"That makes sense," Dawn said as she climbed into the cab of the truck.

"And, hell, I don't know if I *ever* want you calling me Alpha. That would be too weird, you know?"

"You'll always be my annoying big brother, who once puked on my homework."

Cole's ears reddened, and he scowled over at her. "Let's not mention that to the Talons. Or anyone. Ever. Got me?"

She grinned widely, showing teeth. "Sure, honey. Whatever you say."

"You're going to lord that over me for the rest of our lives, aren't you?"

"It's my job as your little sister."

"Hmph." They drove the hour or so to the Talon den in easy conversation, and she leaned back in her seat. All of their territories might back up to one another, but the actual dens were far enough away to give them some privacy. She knew the dens hadn't always been this close, but as the humans spread out, the wolves had been forced to condense.

"So, what do you think you'll end up being when we become a Pack?"

She turned at her brother's question, surprised he'd voiced it at all. "I haven't thought about it. There aren't really any maternal females in the hierarchy."

"You could end up the Heir," he said softly. "I don't have a mate or children yet, and the Heir is usually a direct blood relative."

She shook her head. "I don't think so. I mean, we might end up on our own path as our Pack grows. I know the Redwoods didn't have a Healer for years since she was mated in later, so we probably won't end up with everyone right away. You know? We aren't that big yet."

Cole nodded, his hand tightening on the steering wheel. "I don't know what will happen, but hopefully, some of our generation will finally mate and bring more people in. We need the stability. As for you being a maternal female...well, hell, I don't know why you couldn't be something else in addition to that. Just because the Packs we know don't have one *now* in a place with a title, doesn't mean it can't happen. You never know. And, Dawn? I want you by my side in this. I trust you, and I know you can handle anything."

She wiped a tear from her cheek at his words and shook her head. "Anything you need from me, I'm here."

He reached over with his free hand and squeezed her knee. "Same, Dawny. Same."

She pinched his arm, and he laughed. "We're outside the gates. Stop it with the name, Cole."

"I said I'd try."

"Not hard enough," she mumbled, and he laughed again.

The sentries at the gate waved Cole and her in after taking a look at them, and her wolf relaxed somewhat until they slid through the wards and she found herself within the Talon den. The wards no longer protected wolves from being seen by humans since they were out in the open now, but it didn't allow outsiders in without permission. Now that she and Cole were near a fully functioning and much larger Pack, Dawn couldn't help but be intimidated.

"This could be us one day," Cole whispered.

"That's daunting."

"Well, from what I hear, the Talons weren't always this healthy and whole. They had to work for this. We can, too." There was a determination in his voice that made her wolf stand up at attention. Her brother would be a great Alpha. He'd make mistakes, but he'd learn from them, that was just the kind of man he was. And while the idea of what was to come also made her nervous, she couldn't wait to see him become the man she'd known he could be all her life.

They pulled up in front of a decent-sized house tucked near the center of the den, surrounded by large trees. It made sense that the Alpha's family would be in a place where they'd be near the most people. And their home was one of the largest she'd seen, but since she knew they probably had meetings in their home rather than another building more often than not, that too made sense to her.

The mated pair stood on the front porch, waiting for her and Cole as she and her brother got out of the truck. While Dawn's brother was a large man, he had nothing on Gideon Brentwood. The man *screamed* dominant Alpha. His wide shoulders seemed to take up almost too much room, and the air around him practically sizzled with energy. He had a big beard and fierce eyes, but when he looked down at his wife for a brief moment, she saw the kindness there. That was what made an Alpha. Her wolf leaned forward, even as it bowed its head at his dominance.

And as dominant as Gideon was, Brie was his exact opposite. She was clearly a submissive wolf, but one that was protected and honored like she should be. She smiled widely at her and Cole, and this time, Dawn's wolf bowed its head in respect and with the desire to be petted.

Tears pricked the backs of her eyes, and she wanted to cry. Dawn needed this. Her people needed this. They needed to become a true Pack. Finally.

"Welcome," Brie said, her smile widening. "I'm so glad you're here for dinner and to just talk for a bit. I'm Brie, and this is Gideon."

Gideon wrapped his arm around his mate's shoulders and squeezed. That action softened him again, and made Dawn like him even more. She might be intimidated by the man, but she was finding herself actually liking him, too. She had met most of the Brentwoods over the past year or so when they had come to visit her small den, but Gideon had never come. There was a difference between a visiting wolf and a visiting Alpha in a shifter's den.

"It's good to have you here," Gideon rumbled, his voice deep and growly. She figured his voice was always like that rather than him being angry or annoyed. "Some of the family is inside. Others are either out on patrol or watching the children. We figured since it's your first time over here, we'd keep the babies with their caretakers for the evening, that way, there's not too much noise all at once."

Dawn heard the truth of his statement, but knew that wasn't all of it. She held back any look of disappointment at the fact that she wouldn't be meeting any of the Talon children tonight. She knew it was for the safety of the young ones, so she shouldn't have felt as if it was a blow to her heart. These people didn't know her or Cole that well, and while it might be safe to bring them over for dinner, there were still some boundaries when it came to the safety of children. That just meant she would have to do her best tonight to earn everyone's trust. Because, darn it, it *was* a slight against her to not be trusted enough to be near the Pack's youngest members. She was a maternal wolf with no children to care for, and while unintentional, this was just another hit to her system.

Cole squeezed her hand as if knowing where her thoughts had gone, and she gave him a small smile. The logic of everyone's decisions might make sense, but that didn't mean she had to like it.

"Anyway, come on in. Dinner should be ready soon, but we have a few appetizers out." Brie gestured toward the open front door and held out her hand. Somehow instinctively knowing the protocol, Dawn moved forward and gripped the other woman's hand. Brie's smile brightened, and she squeezed Dawn's hand before leading her inside. Cole followed them with Gideon coming in last. As he was the most dominant wolf among them, it made sense that he would be the one to protect from outside forces while there were other wolves inside to look after his mate. It was all so odd sometimes how their wolves were the ones that led the way rather than the human side, but that's what made them shifters. There was a balance between the two, and what made a wolf more stable and in control was how they took to that balance.

Gideon and Brie's family milled around the large and spacious living room that connected to the open-concept kitchen and dining room. Dawn didn't need to be told that so many of them were Brentwoods as they all looked so much alike it was a little startling. But despite the fact that there were many others in the room, the first person her gaze clashed with was the one man who made her wolf stand at attention and made her want to duck at the same time.

Mitchell leaned against a wall while he talked to the Talon Healer, his cousin, Walker. Dawn had met the Healer a couple of times in the past when he came to give them checkups since he was also a medical doctor. Yet her attention was still only on Mitchell. And from the way he froze with his beer halfway to his lips, she knew his attention was on her, as well. Walker looked between them, brow raised, and Dawn wanted to curse herself for being so obvious when it came to her irrational crush on the growly and brooding Mitchell.

"Let me introduce you to everyone," Brie said, a curious tone in her voice when she caught the looks between Mitchell and Dawn.

Damn it, she wasn't good at hiding her feelings even if she didn't know exactly what she was feeling to begin with.

"Over there is Ryder and his mate Leah." Brie pointed to a slender male and a willowy woman whose energy told Dawn she must be a witch instead of a full human or shifter. Ryder, Dawn knew, was the Heir to the Pack, but wouldn't be once Gideon and Brie's daughter, Fallon, grew up into adulthood.

"Hello," Leah said with a bright smile, and Ryder tipped his head at her in acknowledgement.

"And over there is Brandon with his mates Parker and Avery," Brie continued.

Dawn knew all about those three as their mating and everything that had happened to them in the process was rather public. She waved awkwardly since she didn't like being the center of attention, but Cole went through the room and shook everyone's hands like the Alpha he would be. He was far better at this socializing thing than she was, and she worked at a damn coffee shop.

"And you know Mitchell and Walker." Again, there was that all too curious tone.

Walker nodded at them, while Mitchell stood there, silent and brooding. She honestly didn't know what she'd done to piss him off this time, but she didn't care. He wasn't going to ruin this night for Cole, so she'd just have to ignore the man. He'd spoken to her *once*, and yet he kept glaring in her direction like she'd stolen his car or something.

Well, she wasn't in the mood to deal with him or his moods, so she'd just ignore him. That was how she'd gotten through the past year with her wolf going crazy at just the sight of him.

Once introductions were made, Brie took her over to where Avery and her men were, and they started talking about random day-to-day things like any other normal person would. As soon as Dawn got over the fact that these were wolves of high power and realized she just needed to act normal, she relaxed somewhat.

Later, after they'd eaten an amazing meal that consisted of red meat, lots of potatoes and pasta, and a few veggies, her stomach was full, and her wolf was a bit more relaxed. They ended up moving around the house again, talking in small groups and completely welcoming Cole and Dawn. She figured tonight couldn't have gone better, and she hoped she didn't mess anything up going forward. When she caught sight of a photo of Fallon and who had to be her cousins on their bellies as they crawled around a blanket, Dawn's smile widened, her wolf whining.

Brie narrowed her eyes and snapped her fingers. Dawn took a step back, her gaze lowering. She might be more dominant than Brie, but that didn't mean anything when it came to an Alpha's home.

"I'm sorry, I didn't mean to offend." Crap. She *so* wasn't good at this Pack politics thing.

Brie reached out and lifted Dawn's chin up, her eyes worried. "You didn't. I only snapped because I finally figured out your wolf. I'm sorry, I should have said something as I snapped my fingers like a crazy woman."

Brandon, the Omega of the Pack, leaned forward and sniffed like he was in wolf form as his eyes widened. She'd have thought it rude, but hey, they were wolves, sniffing was what they did.

"You're a maternal," Brandon said slowly before understanding dawned. "And you don't have kids in the Pack yet, do you?"

Dawn shook her head. "No, Cole and I are the youngest wolves for now. There's another wolf, Sam, who is around our age, too. But when we're allowed to create mating bonds again..." She trailed off, not knowing what else needed to be said.

Brie reached out and squeezed her hand. "I'm sorry the children aren't here tonight for you. It must be hard to have a desire to protect and yet nothing *to* protect."

Dawn shrugged. "I'm fine."

"You should talk with Gwen," Walker said as he walked up to their small group. "She's the lead maternal of the Pack and could probably help you once the Centrals grow a bit."

"And I'm sure she could use help at the daycare," Brie put in before holding up her hand at Dawn's protest. "My wolf trusts you, and you'd never be alone on Pack grounds to ruffle anyone's fur. You need balance to be healthy, Dawn, and we all know the Centrals are on their way to becoming a true Pack. You need to be trained."

Dawn blew out a breath and forced a smile, the emotions running through her right then so intense, she wasn't sure she could keep from shaking. These people...they'd accepted her so easily, even after everything they'd been through.

It was a stunning expression of what a Pack should be, and how strong they were.

Thankfully, the conversation turned to something else, and she excused herself, needing air. She walked out to the back porch, knowing she couldn't venture far since this wasn't her den, but she needed the space.

Only as soon as the door snicked shut behind her, she knew she wasn't alone.

Of course, she wasn't alone.

Damn him.

CHAPTER FIVE

Mitchell cursed under his breath as soon as *she* walked outside to the porch. He'd come outside to get away from her scent since it seemed to permeate the small house with the sweet and floral aroma that was all Dawn, and now here she was, invading his space. Again.

He didn't know what it was about her, but he knew he needed to get a handle on whatever was going on. He might act like a bastard most of the time, but he wasn't cruel. Yet right then, he just wanted to yell and scream and get away from her—and he had no fucking clue why. She was so damn close, too. So near, he could feel the heat of her skin against his. He hadn't gone far from the door when he came outside, and now they were only a few inches apart.

"So...I didn't know you'd be out here, or I would have stayed inside. Not that I'm avoiding you per se, it's more that I know if you're out here, then you're probably like me and need some space to breathe or just be, and now here I am, standing in your way and not letting you be alone. So, yes, not avoiding, but I still try to give you a wide berth. Anyway, I can go back inside if you want, and go, uh...just go. Yeah, I'll do that."

She basically said all of that in one breath, and Mitchell had to admire her for that even if it sort of overwhelmed him.

"And now I'm talking too much, I can see it in your eyes. Or like, the corner of your eye since you're not actually looking at me. Anyway, thank you for listening to me ramble. I'll go back in and check on my brother. Oh, and thank you for helping him, by the way. I know you probably have four hundred things to do a day, but coming by the den and checking on Cole when your Alpha can't...well, that's truly just amazing. I hope you see that even if it might just be a duty to you."

She opened her mouth and was either about to take a breath since she hadn't in a while or start talking again. And since Mitchell didn't know how to politely to tell her to shut up since her voice kept sending his wolf into an odd frenzy he couldn't figure out, he did the one thing that came to mind.

Absolutely the most idiotic thing he could have done.

He turned and kissed her.

Hard.

She froze before moaning. She tasted of sweetness and the wine they'd had at dinner. Holy hell, this was a mistake, and yet he couldn't stop kissing her. He cupped her face with one hand, using his other to tug at her hair so her head fell back and he could kiss her deeper. He nipped at her lips, and she let out small groans that went straight to his cock.

As soon as she raked her nails down his back, he knew he had to pull away. Damn it, he hadn't been thinking, but now he couldn't stop what he was doing.

Annoyed, he ripped his hands away from her and pulled his mouth back, his chest heaving as he panted.

"Why did you do that?" she breathed against his lips, her eyes wide, and her mouth parted in that sexy way that made his cock ache and his wolf howl.

"It was the only way to shut you up." A lie, and he knew it was the wrong thing to say as soon as her eyes darkened, her face showing how she closed herself off.

Without another word, she backed away from his touch and quickly walked to the door, going inside without even a backwards glance.

Hell, he *was* an asshole, and he only had himself to blame for his reputation and actions.

"What the hell was that?" Max asked from the darkness.

Mitchell didn't jump, but it was damn close. He hadn't been paying attention to his surroundings, not with Dawn and her delicious scent wrapped around him, so he hadn't noticed his brother stalking up to the porch. Hell, that was dangerous.

Dawn was dangerous.

"Nothing."

"Didn't look like nothing. Looked like you had that very cute little wolf in your arms and your tongue down her throat. Then you said something stupid, and she ran away from you." A pause. "So you did what any Brentwood would do in that situation and messed up."

Considering that was the most he'd heard from his brother in a while, Mitchell should have been happy that Max cared about it enough to comment. Instead, it just sent him over the edge he'd been precariously leaning over for too long when it came to the tantalizing and far too young wolf. Oh, sure, Dawn was an adult, but he'd seen a lot more than she had, and there would always be that gap.

He pushed those thoughts from his head. It didn't matter if there was an age gap at all since he'd already had his chance with a mate and lost it. He didn't get another one, and that meant *no* women for him. It was too much of a betrayal.

The sweet taste of Dawn on his tongue faded to ash, and he swallowed hard, his stomach turning. He'd betrayed Heather by even *thinking* about another woman, and then he'd done the worst thing possible and kissed her.

"I need to go," he growled out. He moved down the stairs and past Max, who narrowed his eyes at him. "Go inside. The others were wondering why you didn't come to dinner." So had Mitchell, but he knew the answer.

"I'm not going in," Max said softly.

Mitchell stopped moving and turned to his brother. "You should. You can't hide out here and be on the outside looking in. It's not good for you."

Max's lips pressed into a thin line, the scars on his face tugging. "You're the one leaving."

"Yeah, because I fucked up. You haven't. Don't do so now by not showing up at all. You saw how Blade reacted at that meeting when Cole's name came up. We need to be a united force and help the kid learn how to be Alpha. He's way too damn young and needs some experience."

"And seeing the monster behind the curtain will help with that?" Max asked, his voice deadpan.

Mitchell stalked up to his brother and growled. "No, damn it. You're not a monster, and I'll kick your ass if you keep calling yourself that. Now, go inside and hug Brie. She misses you." Brie and Max had been good friends before she mated into the Pack, and when she became his Alpha's mate, Max had only gotten closer to her. Now, Mitchell wasn't sure if the two even spoke anymore—not that Brie wasn't trying.

"I'll go in. For her." Max turned and walked up the steps before stopping at the door. "Want me to say anything to Dawn?"

For a moment, there was almost that teasing tone to Max's voice that he'd had for so long. Mitchell swallowed hard through the emotion clogging his throat. "She's fine," he ground out.

"Sure, brother, sure." And with that, Max walked inside to the delight of the others.

Mitchell turned away and started stripping off his shirt. He balled it up in his fist before making his way to one of the large trees that marked the running areas where the wolves could freely hunt. He threw his shirt down, toed off his shoes, and shucked his pants and underwear, leaving him naked under the moonlight with his wolf on edge.

He bent down on all fours near the base of the tree and tugged on the cord that connected him with his wolf. The change wasn't easy, it never was and never would be. When they were children, shifters didn't feel the pain they did when they were adults. It was as if the moon goddess shielded them from that particular part of shifting as soon as they were able to change around two or three years of age until they were strong enough to handle the pain.

The familiar burn slid over him, breaking bones and tearing tendons as his body morphed into a new shape. His face elongated and fur sprouted over his body. He gritted his teeth at the sweet agony before howling, his wolf now fully at the forefront. He panted and shook off any aches before stretching slightly and starting to run. Though it wasn't a full moon, it didn't matter—shifters could transform at any point during the month. It took energy, however, so they couldn't shift over and over again without becoming exhausted. Stronger wolves could usually change quicker and more times throughout the day, but not always. It depended on the individual wolf.

Mitchell ran hard, his paws pounding the dirt and the wind sliding through his fur. He didn't have a place in mind where he wanted to end up, he just knew he had to keep running. If he exhausted himself, then maybe he'd get Dawn out of his system.

Growling at the thought of her, he sped up and let his wolf do the thinking for him. A couple of hours later, he had his clothes in his mouth as he went to his house in wolf form. He used the lower keypad and his paw to get inside since each house was equipped with those now so wolves didn't have to get stuck outside without a way to get in. The door opened with the use of the lower keypad so he didn't have to stand up and somehow use the doorknob.

His body aching, he made the slow change back to human. His body was covered in sweat, and his bones ached. He'd run far too hard considering he had shit to do the next day and wouldn't be able to sleep off all of the aches and pains. He didn't care right then, though. He deserved any discomfort he felt for what he'd done earlier.

Naked, he picked up his clothes and went to the kitchen to grab some cheese from the fridge since he was too tired for anything else. His body needed the protein, and while meat would be better, some cheddar would have to do. He'd been set on running out his energy instead of hunting, so he hadn't caught anything in the woods. He went back to his bedroom, tossed his clothes in the hamper, and swallowed the rest of his snack in one bite before getting into his large shower.

His wolf was exhausted but still whined at him ever so slightly. With a sigh, Mitchell let the hot water roll down his back and focused on the bonds within himself. He'd been feeling disconnected from the Pack that night, and he knew why—he'd shut himself off from what he was feeling for Dawn, and his guilt over Heather. That meant the bonds that connected him to the Pack were stunted, as well. And since he was the Beta of the Pack, those bonds were wound with another set through that connection. His job was to protect the Alpha. That was it in a nutshell. And doing that, he took parts of the job of being in charge of a large group of people and tried to help with the stress of being Alpha. He organized the daily duties of those not on patrols but still needed within the den like mechanics, juveniles that needed to be placed within multiple areas until they found their footing, and training for those going off into different sectors. Gideon, of course, was in charge of it all, but his cousin couldn't do everything, and it was on Mitchell to make sure Gideon wasn't so overwhelmed with inner Pack things that he couldn't focus on the other hundred things on his plate.

As soon as Mitchell opened up again, the Pack bonds pulsated full force, and his knees shook. Their Pack was healthy, but it needed constant guidance and care. He couldn't let distractions like a pretty wolf with biteable lips get in his way.

Determined, he finished showering and dried off before lying down naked on his bed, too tired to even pull back the sheets. His wolf, now as content as it could be, curled up into a ball, and Mitchell fell asleep, the taste of the woman he shouldn't want still on his tongue.

The next morning, after he ate and stretched his sore muscles, he answered messages and headed over to the elder circle. Though wolves never truly aged and always looked like they were in their mid-thirties or so—sometimes younger, sometimes older—some wolves lived for so long that they were slightly disconnected from the rest of the world and the Pack. They'd been through so much in their lives, *seen* so much, that some of them couldn't function properly within normal wolf society.

They might look Mitchell's age, but as soon as one looked into their eyes, they saw the vastness of knowledge. The Talons didn't have a large elder group anymore, not since his uncle, the former Alpha, had destroyed so much of the Pack, but they still had a few wolves that tended to stay away from others. They'd even formed their own council, though they weren't recognized as one anymore, at least not after a few had betrayed Gideon during his initial mating to Brie. They didn't have authority over the Pack like they once did, but they still had the ear of the Alpha—and Mitchell for that matter.

Xavior, the wolf Mitchell had come to see, sat on his porch, a cup of coffee in hand and another on the table next to him. Unlike many of the older wolves, Xavior lived near the other elders, but he worked with the young pups, as well. He'd integrated himself more within the Pack since Gideon became Alpha, and it had only gone to strengthen the den's base. He was also one of the ones who had fought alongside Mitchell during many of the battles over the past few decades.

"Thanks for coming," Xavior said, taking a sip of his coffee.

Mitchell sat down on the rocking chair next to the older man and nodded down at the other cup. Xavior smiled and gestured toward it.

"I know how you like it, pup."

Mitchell snorted then took the mug and sipped. Xavior was right, he *did* know how Mitchell liked his coffee. "I'm not quite a pup."

"Compared to me, everyone is a pup."

"True," Mitchell said with a laugh, though he hadn't known he would be able to achieve levity this morning. "So, you said you needed help with the door panel?" Each house had a palm scanner in addition to normal locks and doorknobs. The biometrics was connected to the lower one for wolves that Mitchell had used the night before.

"It's actually funny," Xavior said with a shrug. "Or it could be that I'm old and I don't understand all the tech you kids use these days."

Mitchell snorted and shook his head. "You're hip, old man. Don't worry."

"Either that or I'll break a hip, am I right?"

They chatted for a few more minutes before Mitchell got up to help Xavier restart the system. It was a two-person job since one had to work on the program while the other set up the palm print. All the while, Mitchell did his best not to meet Xavior's gaze. He was far more dominant than the older wolf so it shouldn't have been a problem, but he knew the elder was much too intuitive.

Only Mitchell's father had known about his mating to Heather. There had been reasons for that under the former regime, and he couldn't go back and change things, but that meant the only other person in the world who knew that Mitchell lost his mate was long buried. Yet he had a feeling Xavior somehow *knew*.

57

The man saw too much, and Mitchell couldn't share the torment that had been his and his alone for thirty-five years.

Fuck, had it been that long? He couldn't quite comprehend that, yet he knew it was the case. He'd lost Heather thirty-five years ago.

Goddess.

What made things worse, was that Dawn hadn't even been *born* yet. Mitchell was over one hundred years old, and Dawn was only in her twenties. Since wolves lived so long, the age gap didn't mean he was an old man to her young ways, but still, he'd lived, loved, and lost, all before she'd even been born.

But why did it matter? Why was he focusing on her like this? It wasn't as if she were his mate. He'd had someone, he'd lost her. And that was that. Yes, others *might* be able to find a second mate along the way, but that wasn't the case here.

He pushed away the voice in his head that reminded him that mating bonds had changed significantly over the past couple of years. Thanks to the Unveiling and other events, it wasn't as easy as it once was to recognize your mate just by scent and awareness. Now, it took a bit longer and was a little harder depending on the couple.

But Dawn wasn't his, damn it. She was just a temptation that made his wolf irrational.

That was it.

Nothing more.

But from the knowing look in Xavior's gaze, Mitchell could tell he was in trouble.

Deep trouble.

CHAPTER SIX

D awn needed to focus on work and not the inner workings of her mind or the fact that she hadn't been able to sleep the night before thanks to a kiss to end all kisses. She'd been kissed before, of course, since she wasn't some lovesick teen, but she'd never been kissed like *that*. He'd made her burn, need, *ache*, and then had pushed her away.

She could understand the pushing, but she couldn't understand *why*. Why had he kissed her like that? Why had he *kept* kissing her like that?

And he hadn't even wanted to do it if his words were anything to go by.

She buried the hurt, her wolf nudging at her as if trying to soothe. If only she could get the feeling of his lips out of her mind. He'd been rough and demanding, yet somehow passionate and caring at the same time. It was a dichotomy that she'd never known he possessed, and now it would be engrained in her mind forever.

"Dawn? You're lost in space again," her co-worker Kev said under his breath. "You doing okay? I can take over for a bit if you need a break."

Kev was a sweet guy who'd asked her out a few times. Whenever she turned him down, he always smiled and said he understood. Now, they were decent friends, though she was always worried he might ask her on a date again. He was about her age and studying ecology at the university when he wasn't working at the coffee shop. He was also fully human and, apparently, a fanboy when it came to the paranormal.

If only he knew how close to the wolf in human's clothing he actually was.

He was also friends with Sam and that made Dawn smile. Hopefully one day Kev would help bring Sam out of his shell since Dawn could only do so much when she herself wasn't fully out of hers.

She shook her head in answer to his question. "I'm fine."

"Really, Dawn, you haven't taken your break yet, and we're not busy. Go take off your apron and sit with your friends. You deserve caffeine and sugar and to not be on your feet for a bit." He winked as he said it, and Dawn let out a sigh.

She had more stamina than he did thanks to her wolf, but she'd never tell him that. Her feet weren't hurting yet, and she could probably stand a few more hours without pain, but she did need the food. Her body burned calories far faster than any human or witch, and since she was hiding in plain sight among the humans, she couldn't eat as much as she wanted to until she got home.

"A bear claw sounds pretty good, actually." She studied the pastry case in front of her. "And maybe that bacon croissant thing." Her wolf perked up at the word bacon, and she held back a smile. Bacon made anyone's day better.

"I'll never know where you put all that food," Kev said with a shake of his head. "But go take your thirty. If we get busy, you'll be around. It's not like you can't just help if you need to."

"Thanks," she said as she untied her apron and stuffed it under the counter. She pulled out her messenger bag and purchased her food and coffee before heading over to the booth in the back where her friends were seated.

She'd met the girls at the coffee shop when they came in for their morning drinks. Each of them either worked close by or stopped at the coffee shop on the way to their job. Normally, none of them could stay and sit, but since it was the weekend, she figured they were hanging out here instead of somewhere else, probably because of her. It just made her feel worse for ducking out on them the night before.

"Hey, guys, have room for one more?"

Aimee's smile brightened, and Dhani scooted over in her side of the booth to make room for Dawn. Cheyenne picked up the stack of dirty plates that had been in the free spot on the table and stood to take them over to the bussing station.

"I can clean those," Dawn said hurriedly.

Cheyenne just raised a brow and walked away with the stack. Dhani let out a laugh and shook her head.

"You're not on duty," Dhani said simply. "And you don't actually have to bus tables, you know. That's what the cute little station is for. People are just lazy when it comes to cleaning up after themselves."

Dawn shrugged and bit into the bacon croissant. Buttery goodness mixed with the maple and bacon exploded on her tongue, and she was pretty sure she almost orgasmed.

"People need a push in the right direction sometimes," Dawn said after she swallowed. "Plus, not all places have the same rules about bussing, so newbies never know what to do."

"Yes, because the signs explaining where to put mugs and plates are so out of the way," Cheyenne said dryly as she sat back down.

"Hey, you can't expect people to actually *read*." Dawn flipped her ponytail over her shoulder, and her friends laughed. Thankfully, they were alone in their little corner; she'd never have said anything like that in front of costumers. Just because she didn't have her apron on at the moment, didn't mean she wasn't still an employee.

"How long is your shift today?" Aimee asked.

Dawn tilted her head and thought about it, then quickly righted herself. Sometimes, she let her wolf mannerism show a little too much for comfort around her friends. They were far more observant than most people, so she always tried to be careful.

"Actually, I'm off in less than an hour." She winced and looked down at her phone. "Pretty silly of me to take a break now that I think about it."

"Not silly, it's the law," Dhani corrected.

"And it's not like you're busy. The morning rush seems to have died down." Cheyenne looked around the shop before picking up her mug and taking a drink of her latte.

"Still," Dawn muttered before eating the last of her bacon pastry. She'd eaten that far too quickly but, apparently, she was hungry. "Anyway, I'm off soon."

"Do you have any plans?" Aimee asked. "We were thinking of heading to that new boutique at the end of

First Street. I probably can't afford anything there, but it's always nice to look around at pretty things."

"Honey, I don't think *any* of us can afford things there," Dhani added with a wink.

That was probably true. Dawn didn't make much as a barista, but it was enough to live on for now since she still lived with her parents—not that her friends knew that exactly. Aimee was a waitress at the local diner and made about as much as Dawn did. Dhani might make a little bit more as an elementary school teacher, but not by much thanks to budget cuts around the state. Cheyenne could have been making more than any of them if she'd gone into business in any other town, but she'd decided to keep her small veterinary clinic open here, and because of that, she barely scraped by. Them coming to her coffee shop was their only indulgence, and even then, her manager let Dawn put the women on her family discount since they were here so often and Dawn's actual family never came in.

She'd needed to keep her other life a secret for everyone's safety, so having them show up would only blow her cover since Cole was out in the open thanks to that damn website where people outed wolves for fun—or what they called "safety and awareness."

She and her friends talked for a few minutes more before Dawn felt Cheyenne's gaze on her.

"What?" she asked self-consciously. "Do I have something on my face?"

"No, but maybe you did last night."

Dawn froze. Like she'd said, her friends were far too observant. "Huh?"

"What Cheyenne is getting around to is that you have that dazed look in your eyes every so often, like you're thinking about a swoon-worthy man," Dhani explained.

Dawn ducked her head and blushed, and her friends laughed good-naturedly.

"Tell us!" Aimee said with a grin. "Who is he? When did it happen? *What* happened?"

"And don't think you can keep secrets from us," Cheyenne said, smiling herself. "We know all and see all."

That wasn't quite the case, but since Dawn was already keeping a huge secret, she might as well tell them what she could about Mitchell. However, she couldn't actually tell them specifically about him since they all knew he was a shifter and putting Dawn and Mitchell together—not that they *were* together, because hell no—would only lead to more awkward questions.

"It's just a guy from around the neighborhood." Well, that was sort of true, in a not sort-of way.

"Yeah? And what did you do with this guy from around the neighborhood?" Dhani waggled her eyebrows, and Dawn couldn't help but laugh.

"Not *that*. We just kissed."

Cheyenne's face fell. "Just a kiss?"

"It must have been a really good kiss if your eyes got all soft," Aimee put in.

Dawn shook her head. "Well, yes, it *was* a good kiss. But it was also a mistake." She bit her lip before continuing. "He was just trying to shut me up, I think."

"Because you ramble adorably, and he wanted to kiss you," Cheyenne corrected. "Are you sure it was a mistake? You don't look all soft-eyed now, as Aimee put it."

"Do I need to kick his ass for you?" Dhani asked. Dawn couldn't help but laugh. For an elementary school teacher, the woman was surprisingly violent when it came to protecting her friends. Then, of course, so was Dawn.

"No ass kicking needed." Dawn paused. "Well, maybe some ass kicking, but I'd just do it myself."

"That's my girl." Cheyenne gave her a nod, and Dawn smiled. "And I'm sorry it won't work out with him, but tell us, was it at least a good kiss?"

Dawn couldn't help but blush, the pink staining her cheeks.

"Damn, must have been a *very* good kiss," Dhani teased.

"Yes, it was a *very* good kiss." A hot, demanding, sweaty, aching kiss that had left her both wanting and cold at the same time when he pushed her away. She didn't know what it all meant, but she knew when a man didn't want to want her. She wouldn't demean herself by thinking that anything else could come from it. Sure, they were attracted to each other, big deal. They were shifters and very sexual beings, but that didn't mean they had sex with every attractive person around them.

Dawn sipped the last of her drink and cleaned up her plates. "I need to go back to work for like twenty minutes, and then I can go shopping if you guys still want to."

"Sounds like a plan." Aimee scrolled through her phone. "There's also that new salad place that's pretty cheap a couple of blocks away from the boutique if we're at all hungry. I know you just ate, but it's not like you had a full meal," Aimee explained.

"There's always the diner," Dhani said with a wink, and Aimee shuddered.

"Please, don't make me eat there," Aimee said with a wince. "Don't get me wrong, the food is good, the place is clean, and it's not that expensive, but my goal in life is to *not* spend my free hours there."

Dawn snorted. "Same, Aimee." She gestured around the coffee shop. "Same. Okay, I'll be back soon if you guys just want to sit here." She looked around the empty place, frowning. For a Sunday before lunch, it was still pretty slow, but she'd already worked over forty hours for the week and wasn't allowed to work any more than that. "It's not as if you're taking the booth away from anyone else."

They waved her away, and Dawn picked up her things and went to the bussing station. Since she was there, she cleaned up the area, traded out an empty bin for the full one, and went back to the kitchen area.

Kev was still manning the front for the few customers that trickled in, so Dawn cleaned up what she could after she put on her apron. Soon, thankfully, her twenty minutes passed.

"I'm done for the day," Dawn said as Kev whipped up a mocha. "Is that okay?"

Kev nodded. "Yep. Gracie should be here soon, but I can handle things myself for a bit. Go and hang out with your friends and get off the clock so you don't piss off Marv." Marv was the owner of the coffee shop. He had bought it from Lenora a couple of years ago. Where Lenora had been sweet and aware that baristas were human beings, Marv was more of a numbers guy. Thankfully, the man didn't come into the shop often, so Dawn didn't have to work with him.

She packed up her things and went to the restroom for a quick touch-up on her lip-gloss and ponytail. And while she was there, she added a little more concealer under her eyes since she hadn't slept well the night before. She'd been so confused and turned on by Mitchell that she'd tossed and turned all night and had ended up with dark circles to show for it. They'd be gone by the evening thanks to her wolf, but she hadn't eaten enough that day to help her heal everything quickly like usual. Since she was a maternal wolf, she actually healed faster than some of the more dominant wolves when she ate well and exercised her wolf regularly. The elders explained that maternals typically healed quickly because they needed to be strong in order to protect pups in times of need. Of course, merely thinking that reminded her that she didn't *have* any pups around to care for.

She sighed and stuffed her things into her bag, annoyed with herself for letting her pity party spiral out of control again. She could continue to volunteer at the daycare center, and Brie had offered for her to spend time with the Talon maternals, as well. That would just have to be enough. And, frankly, it *was* enough.

"Get over yourself," she muttered and rolled her shoulders back. She was going out with her friends to be a normal person for a bit before she went back to her den and dealt with everything else going on. She was strong enough to do it all, she just had to remember to not wallow and dwell on the things she couldn't change.

The girls were standing by the front door when she walked out of the restroom, and she waved as she made her way to them.

"All ready," she said with a smile. "Are we walking or driving?"

"We can walk," Aimee said, and Dawn studied her friend. Aimee looked skinnier than she had before, but when Dawn inhaled, her friend didn't *smell* sick. She had no idea what was going on.

"Are you sure?" Dawn asked softly.

Aimee raised her chin. "Of course. Now, let's go before we miss out on all the super expensive things that we can't afford."

Dhani snorted. "We don't *know* they'll be too expensive."

"Honey, unless it's an outlet or department store with a huge sale, it's going to be too expensive," Cheyenne added dryly.

"Truth," Dawn muttered. "Why are we doing this, then? I mean, it might just make us feel broke and depressed."

Aimee shrugged as they made their way down one of the alleys between the major cross streets where the businesses were. "Because window-shopping can be fun if you're looking for new ideas."

"That is true." Dhani was pretty crafty when it came to making accessories and other things to make an outfit pop.

Dawn was about to say something but closed her mouth, the hairs on the back of her neck rising as her wolf rose to the surface. She tilted her head, trying to understand why she suddenly felt on edge when the scent hit her.

"Run," Dawn growled out low.

Her friends froze and looked at her. "What?" Cheyenne asked. She looked around the alleyway, confusion on her face. "Run?"

"Go," Dawn ordered. "There's something coming."

"What are you talking about?" Dhani asked, her hand going in her bag to lift out a can of pepper spray.

"Just go!"

But it was too late.

A shifter in wolf form pounced on Dawn's back, and she hit the ground face first. The others screamed but didn't run away, as if they didn't want to leave a friend behind. In any other circumstance, she'd have admired that they wanted to fight for her, but this was a *very* large rogue wolf, and they were only humans.

Dawn's claws slashed out as she rolled over. The others gasped, taking steps back as she slashed at the wolf on top of her. She wasn't as strong as he was, and from the look in his eyes, his wolf was out of control. That meant unless she found a way to maneuver around him, there was no way she'd beat him. She might be strong, and had been trained to fight, but she wasn't the best at it.

"Get away from her!" Dhani yelled. "Dawn! Close your eyes!"

Dawn rolled and closed her eyes instinctively as Dhani sprayed the wolf in the face with her pepper spray. While it might have given Dawn a few moments to collect herself to fight back, she knew that it also could have been a mistake. The others started throwing things they found in the alleyway near the dumpster at the wolf, and Dawn shook her head, awed at the fearlessness she saw in her friend's actions—though each of them had stark fear stamped on their faces.

She pulled herself up, her claws out—as well as her secret—and she growled. For some reason, the wolf only wanted her, not her friends. It must have gotten her scent and would only stop or move on once she was injured or dead. That was fine with her, because her friends were human and wouldn't survive this. Dawn wasn't sure *she* would survive this.

The wolf took that moment of hesitation and pounced again. Dawn darted to the side and slashed her claws down its side. It let out a pained howl, and she did it again.

"Get behind me," Dawn yelled, her fangs descending. She was just dominant enough that she could partially shift, but she didn't have time to do a full shift, nor the inclination to be so vulnerable.

"We're not leaving you," Cheyenne yelled. "I'm calling 911."

"Don't, we will handle this on our own," a deep voice growled, and Dawn nearly spun around, startled. Mitchell came to her side, also partially shifted, and she almost let out a relieved breath. Though she hated being the damsel in distress, she was no match for this wolf, and they all knew it. She'd be able to fight and probably hurt the rogue, but not when she was trying to keep her friends safe and wasn't able to shift to full wolf form. She was at a disadvantage, but if she fought alongside Mitchell, she had more of a chance. "Get your friends out of here, Dawn."

"I'm not letting you fight alone," she said quickly. "There's something off with this wolf."

Mitchell spared her a glance, and then things moved quickly. The rogue leapt at them, teeth bared, and she and Mitchell ducked out of the way. While she'd seen Mitchell train with some of the wolves in her den, she'd never seen him move like this before. One moment, he stood next to her, claws out. The next, he was like smoke, drifting from one side of the wolf to the other, tearing through the wolf's fur. The rogue kept coming at her, snapping it's drooling jaws, so she couldn't just run away and leave Mitchell to fight even if she wanted to. It would only follow her, and someone else would get hurt in the process.

She rolled to the side again, aware that her friends hadn't left the alley but were far enough away now to be relatively safe. The rogue came at her again, and this time, she and Mitchell somehow worked as a team, taking the wolf down to the ground. From the manic look in its eyes, she knew there would be no saving it. Somehow, whoever this was had let their wolf take control to the point they'd lost whatever made them sane. They were no longer wolf or human, just pure rogue. Mitchell met her eyes quickly before snapping the wolf's neck in a clean break.

Her hands shook as her claws and fangs receded, and she met Mitchell's gaze once more. He'd saved her and her friends, and she didn't know how to thank him, wasn't sure that he'd accept her thanks anyway. All she knew was that she never wanted to be put in this situation again. She'd train harder, fight harder, and find a way to protect herself so *no one* would have to come to her rescue.

"You fought well," Mitchell growled, his wolf in his voice. "He was so far gone, and a whole lot bigger than you. There was nothing else you could have done. I'll take care of the body, and my team is on the way to clean up. Meet me in your den this afternoon. We need to talk." He paused and gestured over her shoulder, and she turned to see her friends starting at her with wide, hurt eyes. "And I think you need to talk to them, as well."

Dawn swallowed hard as she nodded. She had no idea what she was going to say to them, wasn't sure there was anything to say. Blood covered her hands and arms, and she had a few nicks and scrapes on her cheek and neck. She didn't look like herself, didn't look like a simple barista.

No, she looked like the monster she'd fought to hide.

And now she'd have to explain to her friends why she'd lied to them.

CHAPTER SEVEN

Flashbacks of blood and screams filled Mitchell's mind, and he let out a curse as he made his way to the Centrals' den. He couldn't get over how close Dawn had come to dying just a couple of hours ago in that alley. That rogue had gone for Dawn and only her, no matter that her three friends were easier prey. The fact that Mitchell had been there in the end, as well, should have taken some of the attention off her. The wolf should have focused on the predator in its midst, the one that could end his life. It didn't make much sense to him, and when Kameron showed up with his team, Mitchell said as much.

The wolf hadn't smelled of any Pack Mitchell had been near, but that didn't mean much. When wolves went completely berserk like that, sometimes, their Pack ties severed so severely that even the subtle scent of who they once were washed away in the ebbing panic.

Mitchell's hand tightened on the steering wheel hard enough that it made a creaking sound. Not wanting to break the damn thing, he loosened his grip and let out a breath. He hadn't meant to even *be* near the coffee shop that morning. But Brie and Avery had needed a few things from the bakery next door and didn't have time to make the trip themselves with Avery's new training schedule and the fact that Fallon was going through a not-sleeping phase, which meant that Brie and Gideon weren't sleeping either. And because, apparently, Mitchell was a glutton for punishment, he'd once again offered to go into town for them, knowing he might end up too close to the coffee shop and Dawn's scent for his sanity.

But instead of seeing her work, he'd watched her fight. She'd surprised him with the gracefulness of her moves, but she shouldn't have. She was a maternal dominant and had the instincts to back that up. With more training, she might have beaten the wolf on her own. However, she'd been trying to protect her friends at the same time and had the disadvantage of being in human form while the rogue was fully shifted.

She also hadn't run when Mitchell told her to, but now that he was thinking a little more clearly, he didn't blame her. She was a fighter and wouldn't leave anyone alone against a rogue. She'd worked *with* him, anticipating his moves and fighting alongside him. He wasn't quite sure how he felt about that, but he knew he'd have to train her to fight even better. His wolf wouldn't have it any other way, and since he denied the damn thing everything else in the world these days, he'd give the wolf—and her—that.

He might have felt a bit like an ass, leaving her to talk to her clearly surprised and worried friends, but he wasn't there to comfort her. She was just his trainee, or at least she would be. Nothing more. He'd made sure that one of the soldiers who showed up soon after his call stayed behind to watch out for her. His wolf had pulled at him, not wanting to leave her alone, but Mitchell had been stronger than his need to see to her safety himself.

He hated these feelings, loathed these urges. And he'd be damned if he let himself give in.

Pushing those thoughts from his head so he wouldn't dwell on it for the rest of the day, he pulled up to the Central den and nodded at the single sentry at the gate. The Centrals weren't big enough to have that much of a force protecting their territory, but hopefully, that would change soon. He might talk to Gideon and Kade about helping share resources from the other two Packs until the Centrals got on their feet. He didn't even bother thinking about Blade, as the Aspen Alpha wouldn't even think about it.

The sentry let him inside, and Mitchell drove through the wards, the magic sliding over his skin not as intense as the one at home. That made sense considering there weren't as many members connected to them. He frowned as he parked in front of a grouping of homes. Were *any* truly connected without Pack bonds? He wasn't sure and made a note to himself to ask around later. He didn't know when these wards had shown up in the first place since they hadn't always been there to protect the deserters.

Cole walked out of the small home he shared with his parents and sister and gave Mitchell a nod.

"Thanks for coming by," the future-Alpha said, holding out his hand.

Mitchell reached forward and shook it, easily letting go without a dominance battle. He and Cole each knew where they ranked with each other and also knew that would change once Cole became a true Alpha. At the moment, Mitchell could easily take the kid, but as time progressed, Cole grew stronger by leaps and bounds. Soon, Mitchell wouldn't be sure who would win in a true battle, and his wolf was oddly okay with that. He *wanted* the Centrals to survive, and to do so, they needed an Alpha strong enough to take care of his people. Cole also needed a core group of wolves around him to support his journey. From what Mitchell saw, there were a few around Cole's age—if not a bit older—who could fit that bill. Dawn, to Mitchell's mind, would fit into any role Cole needed. He had no doubt the moon goddess would bless her with *something*. She had such promise.

Promise, once again, that wasn't for Mitchell.

"Are the others ready?" Mitchell asked, his voice rougher than he intended.

Cole gave him a curious look and nodded. "Yes, they're over in the field where we usually train." He paused as if collecting his thoughts. "Thank you for coming to Dawn's aid today." The growl in his voice was unmistakable. "She should have been *safe* with her friends and working, yet some wolf attacked her." The other man balled his hands into fists. "Do you know who it was or why he did it? Or was it just a random attack?"

Mitchell remembered the way the wolf only had eyes for Dawn, even though Mitchell and the others were in the alley with her. That wolf had caught her scent and wanted nothing else. That could have been because the wolf scented her first, and since his mind was broken, he had wanted *only* her...or it could have been something far worse. Since Mitchell didn't have those answers, though, he knew he shouldn't let his mind go down that path.

"Kameron and his team are working on it now. When we have more information, we'll let you know. But I can tell you that the wolf didn't smell of Pack."

Cole's eyes went wolf. "But that doesn't mean anything."

Mitchell gave the other man a tight nod. "True. But Dawn did well."

"Not well enough," Dawn put in as she came up from behind Cole. Mitchell had scented her, but since his wolf seemed to *always* scent her these days, he hadn't known she was so close. "I need to train harder."

Cole wrapped his arm around her shoulders and squeezed. "You're a damn decent fighter already."

"*Decent* doesn't keep me alive," Dawn said with a growl. "I don't want to be the damsel."

Mitchell shook his head. "You weren't a damsel. You'd have fought him off, I think."

"You think." She pressed her lips together.

"Yeah, I think. And don't be angry with me for stepping in. I was *there*. I wasn't just going to walk away because you felt the need to prove yourself."

She pulled away from Cole and snarled at Mitchell. "Did I ask you to walk away? Did I yell at you? No. I'm grateful you were there because we both know that my making it out of that fight alive with my friends unhurt wasn't guaranteed. I'm never going to push away help when I need it. I'm only annoyed that I required it at all. Hence the need for more training."

Mitchell pushed back his wolf, who for some reason, liked the way she fought and growled at him. Now that she was here in front of him, *he* wanted to growl because her scent set him on edge. And he wouldn't be leaving that precipice anytime soon considering that he was going to be the one training her to defend herself and the others around her.

Damn it.

"Fine."

"Fine."

Cole looked between the two of them, brows raised and his wolf in his eyes. "Now that we've got that taken care of, let's head to the field."

"One minute, Cole," Mitchell forced out. "I need to talk to Dawn." He didn't add *alone*, but it was implied.

"It's okay, Cole," Dawn said softly, surprising Mitchell. Cole gave them one hard look before turning around and making his way to the clearing where the training would be held.

"Are you really okay?" Mitchell asked, his voice low. He hadn't meant to ask that, hadn't meant to be with her alone at all. Kameron was the Enforcer and had already asked her things like this. Hell, his cousin had probably already made sure Dawn was fit for training and had every detail from the attack memorized. But that still didn't settle Mitchell's wolf.

Dawn nodded, her eyes not meeting his. He blew out a breath and reined in his wolf since he knew she wasn't dominant enough to meet his eyes if his wolf was so close to the surface. Most people couldn't meet them period, but Dawn was far more dominant than she gave herself credit for. When the Centrals became a true Pack, perhaps the bonds would aid her in seeing that.

"Are you sure?"

She glanced up at him and then looked down again. "Yes, I'm sure. I was scared when it happened, but more so because I wasn't sure if I would be able to get my friends out of that alley in time."

Not knowing what to do with his hands, he stuffed them into the pockets of his jeans. "They looked like they were helping you fight back when I arrived."

She rolled her eyes skyward. "Yep. Idiots. But their pepper spray helped distract the wolf long enough for me to get my bearings and fight back completely." She bit her lip, and he wanted to lick away the sting. "They didn't know I was a wolf," she whispered.

He closed his eyes a moment before letting out a low growl. "Damn. What did they say once I left?"

She shook her head. "Not much." She met his gaze fully, and for the barest moment, he saw the pain in her eyes. "They wanted to make sure I was safe with Kameron, and then they left." Her throat worked as she swallowed hard. "I'm going to talk to them tomorrow...but...but for now, I don't know where we stand. I lied to them for a long time."

"No, you didn't lie. Keeping your true nature to yourself is for your safety and that of your Pack. Of all of us. Just because some of us were forced out into the world doesn't mean all of us had to be." His claws stabbed his fingertips just thinking about how his family had been forced to reveal themselves to the public thanks to the plans of a madman and technology far too intrusive for anyone's good. "You were forced out now in front of your friends, but unless there were other witnesses, Kameron made sure all digital evidence was either destroyed or taken into the Talons' den so we can try to make sense of what happened."

"Yeah, that's what he told me before I left. And while keeping my wolf from the public is one thing, I kept it from my three best friends. I knew that what I was doing was wrong after the Unveiling, and frankly, even before that. It might not be wrong in your eyes, but to me, I should have been willing to trust that they wouldn't walk away once they learned the truth."

She rubbed her temple, and Mitchell wanted to move forward and help her alleviate the tension in her shoulders. He stopped himself, however, knowing he was just going to end up hurting them both in the process. His wolf might have this odd fascination with her, and he might also be attracted to her, but that was it. He couldn't let it become anything more, and giving in to these small little urges he hadn't had in what felt like forever wouldn't change anything.

"I'm sure your friends will forgive you." He wasn't sure at all, but he needed to get to the field and not be alone with her any longer.

She gave him a sad smile and a shrug of her shoulders. "I hope so."

"Let's get to the field, then. You already have more than the basics down, but I'm going to show you how to use an attacker's weight and strength against them. You're not going to grow in height, but you can gain in speed."

"Sounds like a plan."

Yes, it did, and he hoped that he could keep himself and those urges under control long enough for him to teach her how to defend herself. After that, he'd be able to leave and never have to see her again.

It wasn't fair to her, and it damn well wasn't fair to Heather for him to keep prowling around Dawn like this.

Annoyed, he followed Dawn to the clearing and took stock of who had shown up for training. It was part of Mitchell's job within the Talons to work with the soldiers and lieutenants, and here, he would be doing much the same thing. Lieutenants were the wolves who stood guard for the Alpha and were his direct line of defense, the wolves that fought alongside him and his family and the other hierarchy. The Redwoods called them enforcers, but Mitchell wasn't sure what the Centrals would end up calling theirs once Cole became a true Alpha. The lieutenants were the best of the best of those who weren't part of the hierarchy. Soldiers were those dominants that would also be protecting the Pack and would work under their Enforcer. No one had a clear title yet, so everyone was training the same at first and would become more specialized once their talents came out in full force and even more so after the Pack became more defined.

The maternal females like Dawn didn't normally train with the soldiers, but there were only two in the whole Pack, and Dawn was far more dominant than the other woman. The other woman normally trained with the submissives, who still needed to learn how to fight and control their wolves, just not to the extent that the dominants did. Every wolf had his or her place and special skills, and it would be the Central Alpha's and Beta's jobs to ensure they were trained and put in the correct roles.

Training took two hours, and then he called it quits for the day. He had his own duties for the Talons to complete, and he didn't want to tire out the group since most of them had day jobs and shifts for the den. He also needed to get away from Dawn as soon as possible. Her scent wrapped around him, tightening with each bend and sway of her hips. She was a damn good fighter, and if she'd been any other wolf, he'd have helped her more one-on-one, but he forced himself to stay back. Instead, Cole had helped her with things she needed a little more practice on while Mitchell stood back and watched.

There was something terribly wrong with him if he couldn't get this one wolf out of his head, and he didn't want to think too hard about what that could be.

Pushing those thoughts from his mind, he made plans with Cole to come back when he could, and headed to his car, Dawn by his side. The future Alpha had stayed back to talk with his men and woman who would one day help him run the Pack. Dawn, however, had offered to walk Mitchell to his car before she headed to wherever she needed to go.

Once again, this woman was going to kill him.

"Thank you for doing this," Dawn said as she wiped the sweat from her brow with her forearm. "I know you have plenty of other things to do, and coming into a non-Pack to show us how to defend ourselves wasn't on the agenda, but you did it anyway. So, thank you."

He shook his head. "It's what any Pack *should* do. And I know Jasper, the former Beta of the Redwoods, is stopping by, as well." The Redwoods' new generation had recently taken over the hierarchy, but Jasper, one of Mitchell's friends and confidantes, had time on his hands these days to help the Centrals. It didn't hurt that Jasper was also Brie's father and connected to the Talons in that way, as well. With so many connections between the Redwoods and Talons, sometimes it was as if they were one large Pack with two Alphas instead of two distinct groups.

Oddly enough, with all they'd been through, Mitchell didn't mind that as much as he probably should.

"I like Jasper," Dawn said with a smile. "He and his mate are sweet and really do their best to help us figure out what kind of Pack we need to be. Plus, I love the fact that they're also Brie's parents and Fallon's grandparents. You can tell they love their daughter so much, and they still watch over her even though she's mated to an Alpha. There's just so much history there, you know?"

Mitchell nodded, the subject of mates setting him on edge as always. "We all have history," he said slowly. "Some good. Some bad."

The light in her eyes died, and he knew he hadn't said the right thing. She was born into the most infamously traitorous Pack, after all. She knew all about the wrong side of history.

"Shit, I'm sorry."

"Don't be. You didn't mean it like that, and I've spent my whole life the daughter of a Central. Others have it way worse than I do because they were actually alive during the war and have scars some can see, many you can't. I'm just me."

He wasn't aware he was standing right in front of her, the heat of her skin warming his, until he had her cheek in his palm. "I don't think you could ever be just you." Damn it, what was he saying? He needed to get out of there, needed to go home and never look at this woman again.

"Mitchell?"

In answer, he once again proved himself a fucking idiot and kissed her. Unlike before, this wasn't a hot and heavy, barely breathing, needing you kiss. This was softer, tempting, and sweeter.

And because of that, it hurt that much more.

He pulled away, resting his forehead on hers. "Fuck."

"What are we doing?" she asked, her voice small.

The wrong thing.

He didn't say that, though. He'd already been an ass to her once, and she'd done nothing to him except be the tempting woman she was. It wasn't her fault that she wasn't his mate. Wasn't her fault that his mate had died years ago and left him a broken shell of a man who didn't understand how to do anything except walk in the shadows of the life he'd once lived in secret.

"I don't know," he finally answered, his voice equally as soft.

Whatever it was, though, he knew they'd both lay broken and bleeding in the end.

He didn't know any other way.

CHAPTER EIGHT

D awn hadn't slept more than a few scattered minutes the night before, and it wasn't only because of the attack that had left her life and secrets open to those who hadn't known before. The same attack that had put her soul and future on the line. She still couldn't quite believe that Mitchell had kissed her. Again.

And just like before, he'd run away as quickly as he was able as soon as the reality of the situation hit him. Not that Dawn actually *knew* their precise reality since she didn't know why Mitchell fought so hard against wanting her. It wasn't as if she knew him at all.

She only knew the stories she'd heard, the tales of the dominant fighter that had saved so many.

And while she might want to know him better, she wasn't sure that would be a good idea for either of them. She'd seen the darkness in his eyes, the hurt that he'd tried to hide, and she honestly didn't know if she had any right to pry into that. He had gone though what had to be countless horrors with his former

Alpha and then once again after the Unveiling. Who was she to see the man beneath the hard exterior?

Annoyed with herself for becoming so philosophical in the morning without her coffee, she made her way into her kitchen where her mother was making pancakes and bacon, and her father was working on the computer. He worked at all hours of the night as a financial advisor for a major company in the city and was using his expertise in the field to help the Pack. Future children in her den would never have to worry about education and going off to college— their way would be paid with the Pack funds like it was supposed to be. She might even be able to do that once things were a little more settled with the Centrals. With everything being so up in the air, it was hard for her to make any firm plans about who she wanted to be when the dust settled.

Again with the philosophy.

Her wolf shook its head in disgust, and Dawn pushed those thoughts from her mind.

"Hi, baby, breakfast is almost ready."

Dawn leaned forward and kissed her mom's cheek. They were about the same height, and her mother, Mona, only looked a few years older, if that. Soon, they'd look the same age thanks to their shifter genetics.

"Good morning."

Her mom set the spatula down and gave her a bone-crushing hug. "Good morning, baby. I know we didn't get to talk last night, but I'm so happy you're home and safe." She kissed Dawn's cheek before going back to flipping pancakes. "Can you refill your father's cup and maybe, if you're in the mood, make me a mocha? I have the espresso machine set up, but no matter what I do, I can never get it done as good as you."

Dawn smiled and kissed her mother's temple. "I'm a professional, after all." She tried to keep her tone light, and the conversation steered in the direction of coffee instead of the attack. She hated that she'd worried her parents, but it wasn't as if it had been her fault. Her parents trained alongside her most days and knew the dangers of their people. Yesterday, however, was just the first time something had occurred when Dawn was on her own.

"Are the girls coming today?" her father asked when he leaned back in his chair after saying thank you for the refill.

Dawn's wolf stirred, and she nodded before going to make mochas for herself and her mother. They didn't have much money, but Dawn had found an old espresso machine at a thrift shop and gifted it to the household last holiday season.

"Cheyenne, Aimee, and Dhani should be here after lunch. Aimee texted last night and asked if they could come and talk, and I figured it would be a good way to get it all out in the open."

"Your friends are good people," her mother said with a soft smile. "They'll understand why you had to keep your wolf a secret from them. I think they must have just been overwhelmed yesterday with the attack." She blew out a breath. "I'm so proud of you for fighting for yourself. And while I'm glad Mitchell was there in the end, I know you could have done what you needed to do."

Dawn couldn't help but smile. As sweet and cute as her mother looked, there was a fierce predator beneath the skin that spoke of her mother's strength. She'd lived through the Central War, after all, and had come out sane and with her mate by her side. Mona knew how to fight and fight well.

"Thanks for the vote of confidence," Dawn said wryly. "And I'm going to train harder. I don't like how the rogue caught me by surprise."

"I don't like that a wolf was out there to attack you at all," her father snapped, his wolf in his tone. "There's something coming, I can feel it." Her father's wolf was always attuned to the wind—as if it could tell things were off around them before any of the others could. He wasn't a true foreseer like it was rumored one of the Talons was, but he was close.

"What do you mean?" Dawn asked, alert.

Her dad shook his head and pinched the bridge of his nose. "I don't know. I've been having dreams again."

Her mom went to her dad's side and gripped his shoulder. "Rand?"

"It's not just the moon goddess business," her father said slowly. "It's something different. Hell, it feels like more than one thing is coming right now, and I can't really figure it out."

Dawn went back to finishing up the drinks while she tried to process everything her father had said and what he hadn't. Something was coming, all right, but these days, it always felt like that, so she just didn't know. But since there was nothing she could do about it, she would focus on enjoying this time with her parents before she went and met her friends and showed them around her small den.

The Centrals didn't have much, and for good reason, but one day, Dawn hoped they would be a Pack people could respect. That was her one true hope.

Even if it seemed so far out in the distance she couldn't quite comprehend what it would look like.

"Hey, dorky girl," Sam said as he came to stand by her on the porch. "The girls from the coffee shop stopping by today?"

Dawn rolled her eyes and grinned at her friend. "Yep. I'm nervous," she said honestly. And she wanted to speak with Mitchell, too, to talk to him about what had happened before, and yet she knew that might all be a little too much for her at the moment.

"Don't be," Sam said softly. He wrapped his arms around her for a tight hug that soothed her wolf in a different way than even her parents or Mitchell did. "They love you and probably just want to know everything about your life because they're curious and caring."

"What if they hate me?" she whispered.

"They won't. They love you," he repeated.

She let out a breath and leaned against her friend. Sam knew the girls, of course, but she knew he put himself on the outside looking in more often than not. That was just who he was, and one day she hoped he'd put himself out there more, maybe get to know Cheyenne, Dhani, and Aimee a little better. She knew he'd kept his distance because describing his relationship to Dawn was difficult without her friends knowing they were wolves. Plus, knowing too many shifters was always a recipe for disaster when it came to secrets.

But soon...soon there would be no more secrets.

At least not too many.

Sam held her tightly for a moment before saying his goodbyes so Dawn could have her privacy. With a sigh, she headed out toward the edge of the den to meet her friends. She wiped her sweaty palms on her jeans and watched the SUV pull into the small lot right outside the wards. Since the girls had never been there before, and weren't part of a Pack, going through wards the first time could be tricky depending on the person, so it would be easier to walk through them rather than have them drive and possibly end up overwhelmed by magic.

After rolling her shoulders back, Dawn made her way to the lone guard on duty and slid through the wards. Magic tingled on her skin, pressing down in one instant, pulling ever so slightly in another. It called to her wolf, and she knew that part of her home called to her, as well. Once she was through, she blew out a breath and faced the three women who had been part of her life since she first hid among the humans and became an adult.

"Hi," she said softly, stuffing her hands into her pockets. She lowered her head, and if she'd been in wolf form, her tail would have been tucked between her legs.

"Don't look like that," Cheyenne tsked. "We aren't angry."

"We were just surprised," Dhani added. "It's not every day one of your best friends gets attacked by a wolf and shows her claws." Dawn looked up as her friend winked. "Literally."

"Are you okay?" Aimee asked, walking straight to Dawn with her arms outstretched. "You weren't hurt, were you? I can't believe that wolf came out of nowhere and attacked you."

Dawn let her friend hug her as tears slid down her face. "What? You...you guys aren't angry?"

Cheyenne and Dhani came up behind her and hugged her as well so the four of them ended up a huddled mass of tears and limbs.

"No, you dork, we aren't angry that you hid the fact you're a shifter from us," Dhani said in that straight-to-the-point way of hers. "We're angry that someone tried to hurt you and we couldn't do anything to help."

Dawn pulled back and wiped her face, though her friends still circled her. "The pepper spray helped," she countered.

"Not enough," Cheyenne disagreed. "But watching you fight just made me think that I probably need to take a self-defense class. We all do."

"I didn't learn how to fight in a self-defense class," Dawn said softly. "But I'm going to train harder to defend myself anyway."

"Good," Dhani said. "And sure, we can't fight against a wolf coming at us in an alley, but we can at least learn to do *something*."

"The main thing is...we understand." Aimee cupped Dawn's face, tears in her eyes. "I always knew you were keeping something back, but I never thought it was this. I also knew that when you were ready, you would tell us."

"It's not that I didn't trust you guys..."

"It's not about trust," Dhani cut in. "Well, not really. Wolves and witches *just* came out of hiding. And not everybody is out, even now. There're no set rules or even a roadmap for telling your friends where you came from when it's all a little magical. So, we get it. We really do."

"But you guys looked so hurt yesterday."

Cheyenne shook her head. "Shell-shocked would be a better description. Of all the ways to end my workday, finding out my best friend's a shifter while being attacked by another wasn't really something that crossed my mind."

"But now we know, and we'd love for you to tell us more—anything you can," Aimee said. "I'm sure there are still some things that are a secret, and we won't pry."

"Much," Dhani said dryly. "We might a little."

"It's sort of our thing," Cheyenne added, and Dawn laughed.

"That is true," Dawn agreed and ducked when Cheyenne went to slap her on the back of the head.

"Wow," Aimee said softly, her eyes wide. "You move *fast*."

Dawn blushed. "I do, though not as quickly as my brother or many of the other dominant wolves I know, but I've had to hold myself back when I'm working at the coffee shop."

Dhani nodded. "Well, this just means we aren't ever going to run a marathon together. I'd pass out from exhaustion long before you even got winded."

Dawn shook her head, amazed at how well her friends were handling everything. In her wildest dreams, she'd never imagined this would be how her coming out would unfold. She still needed to tell them about her Pack's history, but if they could handle the fact that she got furry every once in a while, they could probably handle the road she and her family were on now.

"You guys surprise me," she said softly, her wolf pressing at her. She'd hated hiding her wolf for as long as she had, and she had a feeling her wolf couldn't wait to show itself off in its full glory. That, however, would have to wait for another day. It was one thing to show off her claws and, soon, her den, it was quite another to reveal to her friends her fully shifted form.

"We love you," Aimee said simply before smiling widely. "Now, will you show us your den? That's what it's called, right? Your home?"

Cheyenne bounced from one foot to the other. "I also have like a zillion questions, but I'll refrain."

Dawn narrowed her eyes even when her lips twitched. "You're going to go all vet on me, aren't you."

The other woman blushed, and the rest of them laughed. "I can't help it. I'm curious by nature."

Dawn wiped her eyes, then froze as another vehicle pulled up next to Cheyenne's SUV. Well, crap, she hadn't been expecting to see him today.

"Is that...?" Aimee trailed off, her voice a whisper.

"Yep," Dawn answered.

"Is he the guy you kissed?" Dhani asked, and Dawn shot her friend a glare.

"Wolf hearing," Dawn mouthed, and Dhani's eyes widened.

"I'm going to take that as a yes," Cheyenne muttered. "So many questions..."

Dawn tried to ignore her friends, but it wasn't that easy since they were going between staring at her and the two men walking toward them. For some reason, Mitchell and his cousin Walker had come to her den, and now they were going to meet her friends. Mitchell had seen the others, of course, the day before, but he hadn't introduced himself considering the event in question.

"Dawn." Mitchell's deep voice slid over her skin, and her wolf stood up, wanting more. Her nipples hardened, and she had to press her legs together just from one word. This man was dangerous for her, and they both knew it.

"Mitchell," she said roughly and then cleared her throat. "Hi, Walker."

Walker looked between the two of them for a moment before giving her a nod. "Dawn," he drawled. The man drawled really well considering he was from up north like the rest of them.

She cleared her throat when her friends stared at her, waiting for introductions. Crap. Mitchell was *not* good for her brain. "This is Cheyenne, Dhani, and Aimee. They're my friends that were with me yesterday. I'm going to show them around the den."

"Nice to meet you," Mitchell said, though she didn't hear much emotion in it. She rarely heard or felt emotion from the man though, unless he'd just pulled his lips away from hers.

Walker didn't answer except to nod, but he had his eyes on Aimee, his gaze unblinking. He studied her friend enough that Dawn shifted from foot to foot, trying to get his attention. He must have realized he was staring because he shook his head and rolled his shoulders back.

The odd thing was, however, that Aimee stared, as well.

Okay, then.

"Have you been through wards before?" Mitchell asked the others.

When they shook their heads, Dawn cut in. "That's why I'm out here. I figured I'd help them through just in case."

"It won't hurt, will it?" Dhani asked, eyeing the space in front of her dubiously. Humans couldn't see the wards, but unlike before the Unveiling, they could see inside to the trees and homes that made up her den.

Situated between two cliff faces, the Central den wasn't all that big. They only had a small area of land that they'd claimed for themselves once they left the Centrals. It bumped up against a large swatch of land that used to be the first Central den. Gone were the homes and buildings that had housed the original wolves that used to live there. When the war ended, and the demon that came to Earth was sent back to

Hell, everything had been razed in a fit of magic. At least, that's what others told her.

Now, the small den they lived in sat between the Redwood and Talon dens at the top corner of their territories. Her people didn't have much, but they had each other, and the beauty that was their den. Her favorite part was the tall waterfall that poured water into their river that circled part of the den. It was gorgeous with its powerful pull and tall, red, rocky edges showcased between the trees far older than she and her family. It spoke of true magic and the power of the earth.

"It shouldn't," Mitchell answered finally, and Dawn pulled herself out of her thoughts. She hadn't meant to go off on a tangent in her head, but she was proud of what her Pack had now, and she wanted to show her friends where she came from.

"Shouldn't?" Dhani asked dryly. "That doesn't sound very reassuring."

"It's magic," Walker answered. "We can't predict how it will affect everyone since we don't know exactly what ties each person has to magic itself. All of you should be fine since you're human, but for all we know, there was a witch in your family generations ago, and you could end up feeling a slight tug or a push as you walk through."

"All I feel when I go through these particular wards is a pull and tug at my wolf," Dawn put in. "It's almost as if it's telling me that I'm home but at a base level. And our wards aren't as strong as the Talons, so these are probably pretty good wards to start with."

"I have so many questions," Cheyenne muttered. "But I'll wait until later before I go through the bullet points."

Dawn shook her head and laughed. "Okay, then. Let's do this. Ready?"

Her friends eyed the space in front of them and nodded one by one. Mitchell went to one side of them while Dawn stood on the other. Walker, a Healer in truth and nature, stood behind them as if ready to catch anyone if they fell.

"It's really not that scary," Dawn said after a moment of silence. "I promise."

"Well, come on in girls, let's see what kind of magic we have," Dhani said with a laugh, and the three of them took a step forward.

The wards weren't all that thick, so it should have only taken a step. Dawn was through in an instant and turned to see Dhani clutching her head and Cheyenne staring at her friend in confusion. Aimee, however, lay against Walker's chest, her face pale and sweaty. Mitchell cursed under his breath and went to help, but then stopped suddenly and looked over his shoulder.

"What?" she asked, then the ground moved beneath her feet. People screamed, and she reached out to hold Dhani's arm to steady the other woman. Dawn's wolf rammed at her, scared and yet wanting to help others at the same time.

Large fissures split the ground, and a tree that stood a few stories high cracked at the base. The sound echoed through the area before the tree, older than her history, toppled to the ground in a deafening roar like thunder. The forest floor rolled and shook, and she fell to her knees, unable to keep her balance. The others did much the same, and soon, she found herself kneeling beside Cheyenne and Dhani with Mitchell on her other side, holding her by the hips as if to steady her. Walker and Aimee sat a few feet away, the Healer's strong arms around her fragile friend as the earth quaked.

Had this been what her father saw? Was this what had been coming for them?

And just as quickly as it had arrived, the earthquake ended, and the world stood still again, silent, waiting.

CHAPTER NINE

Mitchell squeezed Dawn's hips before letting her go, knowing he needed to keep his distance even though his wolf had to make sure she was okay.

An earthquake.

A fucking earthquake.

They weren't uncommon in their area with the dormant volcanoes and fault lines near, but it had been a long while since he'd felt one of this magnitude. And he'd never been out of his den and away from his Pack when it had happened. The bonds that connected him to the others pulsated in fear and worry, but he didn't feel any loss or grief. That was something at least, but his head couldn't quite keep up since he was still holding Dawn in his arms and had no idea of the real damage within any of the dens or the area.

"Are you okay?" he asked, his voice almost a full growl. He'd have pushed back his wolf, but he knew it would only be a lost cause at this point. He'd been fighting his wolf for weeks now, and with the adrenaline currently coursing through his system, there was no way he'd be able to do that again.

She turned in his arms and sat up straight, nodding. "I think so." Her gaze traveled over her arms and legs before turning to him. "You?"

He gave her a tight nod before leaping up to his feet. When he held out his hand, she took it readily and stood up next to him, ever the watchful wolf. She went to check on her friends while he went to Walker's side. His cousin held Aimee in his arms, a frown on his face. Aimee, on the other hand, was trying to pull away from him, but Walker wouldn't let go—very unlike his cousin.

"What's wrong?" Mitchell asked, kneeling down beside them.

"I'm fine," Aimee said, her voice stronger than he'd thought it would be considering she'd almost passed out going through the wards before the earthquake. "Go take care of the others. I just got a little lightheaded."

"You couldn't even stand before the earth moved beneath our feet," Walker countered.

Aimee narrowed her eyes at Walker and pushed. The other man immediately let her go and sighed.

"You need to at least rest. Don't overdo it."

"I'm fine," she repeated, and Mitchell just stared at them, confused. He didn't stop to figure out what was going on between the pair, however; he didn't have time to deal with it right then.

"Everyone good enough? Any injuries?" The others shook their heads, and each was standing on his or her own two feet, though they were all a little paler than they had been before.

"I need to head to the Talons," Walker said quickly, rubbing his hand over his chest. "There are a few injuries." Mitchell's heart sped, but before he could say anything, Walker continued. "Nothing too major, but I still need to go. Can you get back to the den on your own?" Mitchell nodded at the question. While he could go back with his cousin, they both knew that he might be needed here. Walker turned to Dawn. "I know you don't have a Healer yet but—"

Dawn cut in and raised her hand. "Your people come first. And you *know* there are injuries while we don't know anything at the moment."

Walker gave her a tight nod, then looked at Aimee for one long moment before jogging back to his vehicle. Aimee stared after him a bit before turning back to the others as if suddenly realizing they were all staring. Again, though, Mitchell had more important things to worry about.

"That tree might not have been the only one to fall," he began. "I'll check out the rest of the area to see what kind of damage you have."

"I'll go with you," Dawn put in.

"Me, too," Cheyenne added. "I have a med bag in my SUV. Yes, before you ask, I *am* a vet, not a human doctor, but I still have a large first-aid kit for humans, as well. I like being prepared, and I can help with a lot more than anyone who's not in any medical field."

Mitchell nodded at Cheyenne's brisk tone. "Good. We might need you." She ran off to her SUV that was still in sight and got her bag, returning quickly. He turned to Dhani and Aimee. "What about you two?"

"We'll go wherever you need us and stay out of the way if you don't," Dhani answered for them both. "But we have strong hands and are still standing. Just tell us where to go."

Aimee nodded in agreement, and Mitchell blew out a breath. "Let's go, then." He started toward the den center, then veered off at the first shoulder, the four women by his side, ready to face whatever came at them.

The earthquake had taken down a few trees and split the earth in a few places. Gas lines had to be turned off while one of the water mains had to be fixed before it flooded a nearby home. Fractures had appeared in the outer walls of a few newer houses that the Pack was building, but Mitchell figured those wouldn't be too hard to fix since some of them were still in the building stages anyway and had a team around to work on them.

Though not a human doctor, Cheyenne was a blessing to the Pack and helped them with cuts and bruises and even set one bone. Sure, she might have had an easier time if they'd been shifted into their wolf forms, but there were some lines of respect they didn't cross—and treating a shifter like an animal was only one of them. Aimee and Dhani had helped clean things up, fed people, and comforted those who looked a bit shaken. The two of them didn't have the medical skills their friend had or the physical strength of Dawn, but they hadn't backed down or strayed for one moment. Dawn's friend Sam had helped where he could, though he wasn't as strong as some of the other wolves. Mitchell understood the man's relationship with Dawn as one any pack member would have with someone of their Pack and liked that she had someone to lean on.

After a few hours, Cheyenne had finally taken the other women home, and that left Mitchell and Dawn alone while the rest of her family continued to clean up the mess from the earthquake.

Mitchell sighed and looked down at his phone, reading the texts his family had been sending him throughout the day. There had only been a few minor injuries with the Talons, but Walker needed to be there since one of the ones hurt had been a pregnant submissive wolf whose mate was out of the state on business.

"Everything okay at home?" Dawn asked.

"It will be," he growled.

She stood by his side and wiped her hair from her forehead, spreading dirt along the way since both of them were covered in the stuff. Dawn had been right by his side throughout the day, cleaning up what she could and helping lift debris. He'd seen a strength in her that he hadn't known she possessed, but from the way she reacted, he had a feeling this was the true Dawn. Of course, the one that rambled and acted awkward around him might also be the true Dawn. She was most likely an interesting mix of the two, and that made her all the more intriguing to his wolf.

He was beyond the point of fighting the idea of his attraction to her. When he'd seen her fall as the earth shook, his wolf had taken over, and he knew he couldn't lose anyone else around him. He'd already lost his mate and had almost lost his brother and best friend just a few short months ago.

He wasn't sure he could lose Dawn, as well.

And the fact that he felt like that worried him.

There was only one reason he would be feeling like this for someone he wasn't bonded to, and that was something he didn't want to think about.

Something he wasn't sure he could ever say aloud.

Because while the idea of a wolf only having one mate in the world for them might be true in some cases, it wasn't always that way. For each shifter, there were a few potential mates that they could meet in their lifetime. Yes, those potentials were *fated* mates, but that didn't mean the human half was ready to fall in love and continue that journey. The couple—or triad—could walk away and not mate with one another if they so chose. He'd seen it happen a few times in his lifetime when the couple wasn't suited in some sense, like when it came to their dominance and place in the Pack or the personalities of their human halves just didn't fit. Other times, it was because one of the pair was in love with another, even though they weren't mates. In those cases, a mating bond might form years later once the couple proved to their wolves that they were made for each other, but Mitchell had only heard of that happening once.

His wolf paced, and he tried not to let any of his thoughts show on his face. He hadn't been in either of those situations, and his wolf hated him all the more for it.

He'd found his mate, the first potential he met, and bonded with her. They'd clinched their bond with his wolf when he marked her shoulder after they sealed their human halves by making love where he spilled his seed within her.

Heather was the only potential mate he'd ever met because once the mating bond took hold, his wolf didn't recognize anyone else. That was how fate worked even if it took free will to enact it.

But Mitchell had a feeling he'd met his second potential mate because he didn't have a bond anymore to Heather. That had broken when she took her last breath, tearing through him and fracturing his soul in the process. He wasn't fully sure, however, because ever since the paranormal world had changed with the addition of human interaction and manmade magic, sensing one's mate wasn't as easy as it used to be for some people.

But Mitchell knew.

Dawn could be his mate.

He also knew he couldn't do anything about it.

He was a fucking asshole, just like he'd made others believe.

"Mitchell?"

He shook himself out of his thoughts and looked down at Dawn. "Yes?"

"Are you okay? You looked lost in thought."

If she only knew.

"I'm fine. You?" He turned and looked at her fully. She'd been solid and a symbol of strength throughout the day, but he could see the toll it had taken on her. The fact that she'd been afraid for her friends and people during the quake and then witnessing the aftereffects of destruction had pushed her to her limit. Her wolf had been in survival mode, driving her to care for everyone, and she'd neglected to take care of herself. And though Mitchell *knew* he couldn't give in, he also couldn't stand to see her shaking when she had no idea she was even doing it.

"I'm fine." He'd have believed her if her teeth weren't chattering as she said it.

"Let's go for a walk," he said after a moment, hoping he wasn't making a monumental mistake.

"A walk?"

He took her hand and pulled her toward a grouping of trees that was still in the den but away from people. The others didn't need to see Dawn let go and show weakness. She might not be the future Alpha, but she was of his family, and someone that the others looked to. Yes, she was the youngest, but that didn't mean much to wolves who led such long lives. She had an air about her that spoke of strength and that maternal dominance that drove her to care for people.

"Where are we going?" she asked. "And don't you need to get back to the Talons? I'm sure they need you."

"My family's taking care of them." He waved his phone with one hand as he still held her with his other. "If they need me, they'll let me know, and I'll be there. But right now, you need me."

He wanted to bite off his tongue at that remark, and from the way she raised her brow at him, he knew he'd probably overstepped. Thankfully, they reached an area that had a small meadow of lush grass, which was concealed by large trees that strained against one another to reach for the sky. He'd spotted the area a few weeks ago when he and Cole went on a run, and he knew that it was secluded enough that Dawn could lose the shell she wore for others and break down if she needed.

"We're alone now," he whispered softly, bringing her to his chest. He knew he shouldn't be doing this since it wasn't fair to her, but his wolf needed to know she was close, and hell, she needed comfort, too. "You can let go."

She shuddered in his hold, tears sliding down her cheeks. "I was so scared. We're not that big of a Pack, and I don't know what I'd do if I lost any of them. Everything could have been so much worse."

He rested his chin on the top of her head. "But it wasn't. And you and Cole did great today with them. You helped where needed and were a symbol of what your Pack could be."

She blew out a breath, wiping her face while still in his arms. "I hate feeling weak."

"You aren't weak."

"You say that, but you're holding me because I need it."

"You do. All wolves need touch. Comfort."

"You never need to be held."

He did, but he didn't say that. Instead, he held her closer, letting the sounds of the forest wash over them as both of their wolves calmed down. At least, he hoped his wolf would calm down, but with her intoxicating scent wrapped around him like a tight glove, his wolf was on a new kind of edge—one where he wasn't sure what he would do about it.

"Mitchell?" Dawn's voice was quiet, but it didn't shake.

He stiffened. "Yes?"

"What are we doing?" she asked again. She'd asked before, but he hadn't answered honestly. Of course, he had no idea what they were doing, so it wasn't as if he could truly reply.

"I don't know," he finally said, as honest as he could be. He slid his hands through her hair, and his wolf growled at him.

"That's not a good enough answer." She wasn't looking at him but still held onto him as tightly as he did her.

"I'm not a good bet," he growled out. "I'm...I'm not going to be your mate."

She backed up slightly so she could look him in the face. "Did I ask you to be?"

His claws pricked at his skin, his wolf pushing at him, and he shook his head. "No, but this attraction? If we aren't careful, it could lead to the one thing I can't do."

"Are you going to tell me why?"

"I can't." His voice didn't break, but it was close.

"I can respect that," she said, surprising the hell out of him. "We all have our reasons and secrets. But, Mitchell? I never said I wanted a mate. I *don't*."

"You say that now..."

"Don't put words into my mouth, Mitchell Brentwood. You might be older, but you don't know what I'm thinking or feeling. There's attraction between us, that's for sure, but we don't have to do anything about it. Or, we can let our hormones rule for just this instant and know that there's no future. We're shifters. We're sexual creatures and need touch to survive. So, we could give in to this temptation and know that nothing will come of it. And, frankly, that's okay with me. I don't want a mate. I'm not ready for one, and I sure as hell don't want one who wants nothing to do with that level of bonding."

He blinked at her, surprised as hell by her words yet turned on at the same time. "I don't want to hurt you." He didn't want to hurt himself either. He couldn't get too close. Because if he did, and he ended up losing her, he'd break what was left of him. As it was, there wasn't that much to give.

She shook her head even as her teeth pressed into her lip. "You're not going to. But we can't keep dancing around each other, kissing like we can't get enough of one another and then hiding from it. We're both here. We're both adults." She blew out a breath. "I'm not a virgin, you know. I *have* had sexual relationships before."

He held back a growl, annoyed with himself for feeling any jealousy for a man he didn't know. "Don't talk about other men when you're in my arms."

She snorted. "You're getting all growly, and yet you're keeping yourself at a distance. My wolf wants you, Mitchell, and heck, so does the human part of me. We don't have to hold back from one another, not completely. And for all we know, we're not even potentials since mating bonds are so murky nowadays. We'll be careful."

"I don't have a condom," he bit out. "No marking, that's something we can control. But once I'm inside you, I don't know if I'll be strong enough to pull out. That's not safe anyway." They didn't have diseases since they were shifters, and they couldn't have children unless they were mated, but once he came inside her, he had a feeling the start of the mating bond would let its presence be known.

She bit her lip and tugged at the messenger bag she'd been wearing throughout the day. "I have one in my wallet."

He blinked at her, surprised but eager. His wolf was damn ready, and hell, so was the man.

"I've uh...never been with a wolf before, and it's always good to have protection with humans especially when you're hiding who you are. I keep a couple on me in case I'm ever in a situation with a guy I like—"

He kissed her hard, stopping her words. "*Never* feel like you need to justify being safe to me." He kissed her again. "No promises?" he asked, knowing he would probably hurt them both.

"Just help me *feel*." She bit his chin, and his dick hardened more. "After yesterday and today...I need to *feel*."

She wasn't alone, and damn it, he couldn't hold back anymore. He'd been refusing himself for so long, denying who he was and what she could be *with* him, that he had to give in.

So he leaned close and pressed his lips to hers, craving, needing, demanding. Her nails dug into his chest, and he growled, deepening the kiss while tugging at her hair so he could pull her head back slightly.

"Just us," he growled into her mouth. "You and me. Just..." He couldn't say "no strings" because that would be a lie, and he wasn't that much of a bastard, but he wasn't sure what else he could say.

"I get it." She bit his lip. "Stop worrying about hurting me and make me *feel*."

Wordlessly, he picked her up by her waist and kissed her harder, his breath coming in pants, and his cock straining at his jeans. She wrapped her legs around him, and he walked over to the nearby tree that shaded the small patch of grass they were on and pressed her into it.

"Am I hurting you?" he asked, licking down her neck and shoulder.

"No. I need...I need..." She couldn't seem to voice what she needed, but when she arched her hips into him he got the idea.

So he tugged her closer while keeping his mouth on her and then laid them both down on the ground. He knelt above her and stripped off his shirt, needing skin-to-skin contact. Dawn sat up so she was right underneath him and slowly ran her hand down his chest before leaning forward and kissing right beneath his heart.

He froze, his wolf rising at the touch of her soft lips against his skin. When she looked up and met his gaze before looking down just a little at the three scars on his pec, he sucked in a breath. Since he was a shifter and got shirtless before shifting and when he worked outside in the heat, he'd never hidden the scars. However, no one had ever touched them beyond when he fought or trained and it was an accident. Dawn hadn't touched him either just then, but it was close enough to make him freeze.

The three jagged scars were right over his heart, and he still remembered the exact day he got them. He knew the empty hole that he'd been trying to dig out when he sliced through his own flesh, trying to tear out what hurt the most.

His heart.

He hadn't succeeded, but damn if some days he didn't wish he had.

"I'm sorry," Dawn whispered, bringing him back to the present.

He shook his head. "Don't be. They're just scars." A lie, but one he wished was the truth. "Keep touching me." It was an order, but from the way her eyes darkened, he knew she liked it.

He slid his shirt underneath her before pressing her down to the ground and slowly working his way down her body. He nibbled and sucked over her clothes before stripping her completely. Bare before him, she was a goddess. Long, lean lines with breasts big enough to overfill his large hands, and hips that flared out just enough for him to grab onto later so he could fill her to the brim. His cock ached, but he didn't release himself from the confines of his jeans. Instead, he lowered himself over her and gently bit down on her nipple.

She slid her hand through his hair while keeping herself upright slightly with her other arm. He growled low, the sensation vibrating through them both. He sucked one nipple into his mouth while palming her other breast, loving the way she so easily responded to his touch. It had been what felt like forever since he'd had the warm touch of a woman beneath him, and he wasn't going to waste this time worrying about what would happen next.

That would come later.

After giving his attention to her other breast, he lowered himself even more down her body, kissing her stomach and hips before kneeling between her legs.

"I need to taste you," he growled.

Her eyes widened. "Uh...I've never..."

His wolf growled at that, and the human half of him relished her words. He would be the *first*. He was officially a caveman, and he didn't care. "Your humans never wanted to eat you out? Never sucked on this clit of yours as it peeks out of its little hood?" He ran his thumb over her, pressing down on the little nub as he spoke. They both groaned when she arched her hips into his hand.

"They said they didn't like it."

"Fools." He shook his head. "Making a woman come with your mouth is one of the sexiest things in the known universe." He lowered his head and lapped at her with his tongue. She arched again, moaning his name. "So fucking sweet." He kissed his way around her before flicking his tongue over and over against her clit. He hummed low while using his fingers to tease her entrance. He knew she was close to coming the moment he slid one finger inside her wet heat. "Come, Dawn. Come around my finger and on my face." He sucked harder on her clit, and she screamed, pressing her pussy right against him as her inner walls clamped down around him.

Before she could finish coming down from her peak, however, he quickly stripped out of his jeans, careful not to fall over like an idiot in his hurry, then slid the single condom they'd found over his dick and leaned over to flip her onto her hands and knees.

"This position okay?" he growled out, his cock so hard he was afraid he'd burst at the first feel of her.

She nodded, but he needed to hear her words. He tugged on her hair slightly, forcing her gaze to his.

"Words, baby. I need your words."

"Yes, I'm good like this." She swallowed hard. "You made me a nest with our clothes to protect my knees. Now, *please*, I need you inside me."

He growled, positioned himself at her entrance, and pushed deeply inside. His body shook at the feel of her all warm and tight around him, and he had to hold his wolf back from wanting to take over and go harder and faster.

There was just something about the woman in his arms that made him want to lose control.

"Ready for me to move?" he asked, his voice a low growl.

In answer, she moved backward, pressing her sweet curves right against his hips. "Move. Now."

He couldn't help but grin at her tone. For as soft and sweet as she was, she was no submissive. She gave as hard as she got, and now that Mitchell was inside her, he was afraid he'd never want to leave.

Too far.

Don't hurt her.

Don't forget what you lost.

He pushed aside those thoughts and pulled out of her before slamming back in. They both growled, and he kept up the pace, the demanding rhythm he knew would send them both over the edge too soon.

Knowing that with her on all fours in front of him and him going deeper with each stroke it would be too much, he pulled out again, and this time, rolled over onto his back, bringing her with him.

"Ride me," he growled, his wolf in his tone.

She bit her lip as she slid herself over his length, rocking her hips as soon as she was fully seated. If he'd thought she felt good before...goddess help him. From this position, he could see the way her breasts bounced as she rode him, how her hair blew in the wind when she threw back her head and gave him everything.

He thrust in and out of her from below, his cock straining within the condom. "Eyes. I need your eyes."

She looked down at him, her face flushed, and her lips parted. "I'm going to come again."

"Now." And as soon as she arched her hips, one hand on her breast, the other on his chest, he came with her, filling the condom instead of her like he could have done with any other shifter.

Because there had been a reason they used a condom just then. Something neither of them had wanted to leave to chance.

The same reason that left him in a cold sweat instead of the heated haze he should have been in with a limp and sated Dawn sprawled over his chest.

"I need to go," he said softly, one hand on her back, the other on her butt, keeping her steady. It was a shit thing to say when he was still inside her, but it was all too much.

He hadn't been with a woman since Heather. Hadn't come with anyone or anything but his hand in so long, he was surprised he still knew the moves. And now he was wrapped around a woman that could easily break him if he gave her a chance.

He'd already shattered once before.

He wasn't sure he could do it again.

Dawn sat up, confusion on her face for a bare instant before she nodded and slid off him.

"You should check on your den." It was an easy out, but she was the kind of woman who would give him that.

He didn't deserve her, didn't merit anything she could give. "I can walk you home."

She shook her head and gathered up her clothes. "No...no I don't think that would be a good idea."

When she blew out a breath, he wanted to wound himself and add another scar rather than hurt her like he was, but he could barely breathe. The cascading hurt at what he'd done, at how he'd betrayed his mate by laying with another woman slammed into him with such force, he knew he needed to get control of his emotions.

This wasn't Dawn's fault, and there had been a reason he'd stayed away for so long. And yet... he couldn't help but lean forward and kiss her softly. He couldn't hurt her, not when she'd done nothing out of anger or to hurt him. She was just that amazing, and he couldn't walk away now and leave her cold in the forest.

"I'm going to walk you at least to the edge of the trees," he said softly. "And then later, we can talk." He swallowed hard. "I just need..." He couldn't finish his thoughts, but Dawn leaned into his hand when he cupped her face and gave him a sad smile.

"I need time to think, too. I get it, Mitchell. I do. Don't beat yourself up."

And with that, she began getting dressed as he did the same, taking care of the condom with a tissue he had in his pocket before reaching out and sliding his hand over hers.

He honestly had no idea what he was doing, and he knew that they would both end up hurt and fractured in the end, yet he couldn't stay away. His wolf pushed at him even as it wanted to hide from what Dawn could mean to them, and that just meant the human half of him was even more confused.

His time with her just then had rocked his world, just like the earthquake had done earlier.

And now he had to live with the consequences.

Again.

AIMEE

Aimee twisted to the side and stared at the bruises forming on her ribcage. She'd fallen hard on Walker's chest after she collapsed through the wards, but she hadn't thought she would end up with so many black and blue marks because of it.

She had no idea why she'd reacted like she did when she walked through the wards that stood to protect Dawn's family.

She had no idea why she bruised so easily these days.

She had no idea why she was so tired and sick all the time.

She had no idea why everything seemed to be crushing down on her all at once so she couldn't breathe.

Aimee lowered her shirt and leaned down over her sink so she could splash cold water on her face. The coolness shocked her system just enough to add a slight boost of energy that she so desperately needed. No matter how many vitamins and supplements she took, she never seemed to catch up. She'd seen doctors and specialists, and they told her over and over again that there was nothing wrong with her.

Yet she knew there was.

There had to be.

And Aimee didn't know how long she would be able to put the fake smile on her face and keep going.

She was just so *tired*.

Her fingers brushed along her side again, and she remembered the hard chest she'd fallen on.

Walker.

There was just something about him...

And yet she knew it wouldn't lead to anything. It couldn't.

She didn't have the kind of time it would take to find out who the man beneath her touch was.

She didn't have any kind of time at all.

WALKER

Walker held Fallon to his chest and tried to soothe her cries. While shifters didn't get as many diseases as humans since their immune systems were stronger, babies still got colicky. As a Healer, it killed him that he couldn't make everything go away and end up with perfectly happy and healthy babies, but his powers could at least soothe the ache so his future Alpha could sleep.

Of course, that meant the *current* Alpha and his mate would be able to sleep eventually, as well. As of now, Brie was finally asleep, though she'd put up a good fight to stay awake for her baby girl. Walker figured she was able to let go enough to let her eyes close because her growling mate stood by Walker's side, watching every move he made while Fallon cried herself—hopefully—to sleep.

Walker swayed side to side, the ties that connected him to Fallon, as well as his Healer bonds wrapping around the little girl to soothe her lungs and aching throat. After a few more minutes of swaying and singing softly under his breath, the little girl drifted off, the fist wrapped in his shirt loosening its grip.

Gideon took his daughter from Walker in the next instant, holding her to his chest. The little girl let out a tiny growl before resting her cheek on the bare skin peeking out at Gideon's collar and then falling back to sleep with a small smile on her face.

"Thank you," Gideon mouthed, and Walker gave his brother a nod before picking up his stuff and heading out of the house. He'd had a long day, and knew he needed to rest and refill his energy stores if he wanted to stay upright and do his job tomorrow.

He rubbed the back of his neck and headed back to his place. He'd gone to the Centrals' today to help train others and hadn't been able to do what he planned. He might go back tomorrow, but it depended on how things went in the morning with those who had been injured within his own den during the earthquake. They had a lot to clean up as well, and he didn't want to leave those in need. He just didn't like the fact that he hadn't been able to live up to his promises—yet. So when he could, he'd go back to the den and help Dawn's people.

Of course, thinking about Dawn made him think of her friends. He'd reacted strongly to one of them in particular, but he didn't know why. Maybe he just saw things that weren't there since she hadn't seemed as affected as he did.

Maybe he was just lonely. He was one of the few of his direct family without a mate since the rest of them were finding theirs one after another. It wasn't that he wanted to be alone and mateless like so many of his family had seemed to want before they found theirs. Walker actually *wanted* a mate. He just hadn't found her.

Before he could let those thoughts go further in that direction, however, he noticed Mitchell stalking back to his house, his wolf in his eyes for the brief moment the two men saw each other. Mitchell nodded once before slamming his door behind him, and Walker let out a sigh.

His cousin and Beta looked angry, sated, and broken all at the same time. Well, hell, it seemed that Mitchell and Dawn might have finally done something about the attraction Walker had seen between the two. He didn't know what had held his cousin back, though. And he didn't know what was *keeping* him back now. Because if the two had mated fully, Walker would have felt Dawn within the Pack. That's how matings worked.

But, again, Walker didn't know.

He didn't seem to know much these days.

CHAPTER TEN

D awn didn't have to work that day, so instead of staying home with her family and working on things for the den, she decided to do something for herself and meet with Gwen from the Talons. She'd almost backed out twice, but Cole had pushed her out of the house—literally.

She was surprised he hadn't hog-tied and tossed her in the back of his truck before dropping her off at the Talon den himself. And because he'd been so adamant that she take care of her wolf and her future, she'd known it would be okay to actually do it and not put others first for once.

So, here she was, driving through the open Talon gate and wards after being waved in by the sentries on duty. The magic within the wards pushed and pulled at her like the Centrals', but at a higher frequency. Mitchell had been correct in saying that his wards were much stronger. One day, she hoped hers would be just like these, protective and a show of pure strength and the Pack's connection to the moon goddess.

Dawn pulled into the visitor parking lot and shut off the engine. She could have kept driving to the area where she would be meeting Gwen and some of the other maternals, but she figured it would be better to walk through the area and let them see and scent her. Being a strange wolf in a den not of her own meant she needed to be careful. She didn't think the Talons would attack her, but she also didn't want to ruffle their wolves. It was the maternal in her.

Of course, even as her mind went through all of this, she also thought about three nights prior with a certain wolf who had sent her over the edge multiple times and made her crave something she'd never wanted to desire.

Had sleeping with Mitchell been a mistake?

No, she couldn't say that. She'd gone into her life and what she'd done with Mitchell knowing that she'd have to take responsibility for any emotions that might come as a result. She just didn't know what she would do with the fact that her need for him hadn't been fully sated and now she had these...feelings. Feelings she couldn't figure out and wasn't sure if she wanted to.

She had no idea what she was going to do when she saw him next, didn't know if they would even acknowledge what had happened, but since she was in his den, there was a high probability she'd see him today. They hadn't talked since they parted ways that night, but she hadn't expected anything different. They'd both needed to clean up their dens after the quake, and she had to work at the coffee shop, pretending as if nothing had happened in an alley a few short feet away from her place of business. She still had no idea why that rogue had attacked her, but that was just one more thing that kept spinning in her mind while she tried to get through her day.

All of that went on the backburner, though, when she slid out of her vehicle and saw Gwen standing a few feet away. The other wolf smiled widely and waved before making her way over. She'd never met Gwen before, but Brie had given her a description, and the Alpha's mate must have done the same for Gwen since the other woman seemed to recognize Dawn so easily. Gwen's wolf smelled of strength and caring and seemed to be around the same dominance level as Dawn's, though it was a little more difficult to sense that since they weren't in the same Pack.

"Dawn? I'm glad you could make it today." The other woman hugged her tightly, and Dawn inhaled, the scent of Pack—even if it wasn't her own—soothing her nerves. "You ready to learn a little bit about what we do?"

Dawn nodded. "Thank you for having me, and totally. I mean, I *know* I'm a maternal dominant, but it's not like I've ever really done anything with it."

Gwen gestured in front of her. "Then let's make our way to the daycare. Brie will meet us there since she likes Fallon to interact with the younger ones, and she has a fondness for children that tells me if she weren't a submissive, she'd have been the kind of wolf we are. As for not having any experience, I have a feeling you know more than you think you do. Brie told me you work at the human daycare, which totally helps, and I bet the way you interact with your family, friends, and Pack goes down a path of caring and soothing more than others would ever know."

Dawn smiled and shook her head. "You know, I never truly thought about it that way until I talked to Mitchell about it. Hearing him speak about how the Pack works really opened my eyes."

Gwen's eyes went bright with curiosity at the mention of Mitchell, and Dawn wanted to curse. She hadn't meant to bring him up, but it wasn't like she could help it. He *was* most of her interaction with the Talons at this point, and she wasn't sure if she and Mitchell were hiding what they did. The idea of keeping it a secret made her feel like what they shared was shameful, and that wasn't the case. Of course, she wasn't about to tell everyone all the details either. There was a difference between actively hiding something and at least acknowledging that it happened.

"I heard Mitchell was helping out in your den." Gwen shook her head at Dawn's pointed look and began telling her about the area they were walking in and some of the history of the den. Dawn knew the Talons had gone through hell before Gideon became Alpha, but from the deep and aged hurt in Gwen's tone, it must have been a horrific time within these wards.

"And here we are," Gwen said, her arms outstretched. "The kids are playing outside today since it's so nice out, so we can just go through the side gate here. Not everyone brings their children to the center since they aren't all on shift at the same time or have a job outside the den, but most of them bring their pups in a few times a week anyway since interaction while young is essential."

Dawn nodded, a smile playing on her lips at the sound of yips, barks, and laughter. "I had that with Cole."

Gwen wrapped her arm around Dawn's shoulders tightly. "You needed more. We all do. But I'm glad that you had him. Now, you'll have us to help you along. You're not done growing yet."

Dawn snorted. "Uh, sorry to break it to you, but I'm not a teenager anymore."

"No, but everyone's a kid to me sometimes." The woman winked before leading Dawn to the side of the building where all the pups were.

Dawn's wolf preened at the sudden attention of so many children, and she almost went to her knees in relief. This wasn't her den, wasn't her Pack, but she was *home*.

She rolled around with the children in her human form and laughed when they tried to climb up her body, their little paws sliding over her skin since their claws were sheathed.

When Brie and Fallon showed up, Dawn smiled widely from the bottom of a pile of pups before laughing as the little wolves ran up to Brie, barking, and yipping. She stood up and dusted off the dirt from her clothes and then sucked in a breath when a familiar scent hit her nostrils.

"Mitchell!" Brie said with a grin. "I'm so glad you're here. Gideon said he'd be on his way soon."

"My cousin is coming to roll around with the pups, isn't he?" Mitchell asked dryly. He didn't say a word to Dawn, but he stood right next to her and brushed his hand along hers. He may not have done it consciously, but her wolf calmed at the touch nonetheless.

She had no idea what any of it meant, but she knew things were about to get interesting since Brie had caught the movement.

"Of course, he is," Brie answered with a laugh. "Who can say no to pups?"

"Should I get out of the way?" Dawn asked. "I mean, I don't want to overwhelm anyone." One of the younger pups, who had probably just learned to shift, scrambled over to her and nipped at her shoes since he couldn't climb up her legs without using his claws. She bent over and picked up him, nuzzling her face into his fur. He licked her chin before yawning, his mouth opening wide. Then he leaned into her and fell asleep in the next instant.

"Ah, to be a pup," Mitchell muttered, and she looked over at him.

"Hmm?"

"I can never fall asleep that fast. Pups can do it anywhere and everywhere."

She tucked that piece of knowledge into the back of her mind since she seemed to be taking each of the slivers she learned and hoarding them.

Gideon showed up soon after, and Dawn once again almost buckled under the strength of the man's wolf. Mitchell was a strong wolf. Cole was a strong wolf. Gideon? There was nothing to compare...though she'd never met Blade or Kade, the Alphas of the other two Packs in the surrounding territories.

Dawn didn't know what to do with herself, so she left Mitchell's side—something she oddly didn't want to do—and went to sit with Gwen and the children. She was in the middle of helping one of the little girls button up her jumper after she shifted back into human form when Gideon got a call that made the hairs on her neck stood up.

"Mitchell, with me," the Alpha ordered. "We have a guest at the front gate. Brie, will you come with me also?"

His mate nodded and put her hand on his stomach. "Of course. Gwen, can you take Fallon for a bit?"

The other woman nodded. "Of course."

Gideon gave Dawn an odd look before nodding. "Will you come, as well, Dawn? I know I'm not your Alpha, but I think in lieu of Cole, you should be with me. Something tells me this could be important."

Dawn blinked, surprised. "Sure. Of course. Whatever you need me to do." She wasn't sure why *she* would be important when it came to meeting a guest at the gate, but if they needed her, she was there."

Mitchell frowned, and she almost let the hurt get to her before he came to her and held out his hand to help her up. "Kameron texted me who it is, so stay by my side."

Her eyes widened. "Do you think it could get dangerous?"

"I think that you are still training and you should stay by my side. Brie will be by Gideon's."

Dawn wasn't sure what he meant by that since she wasn't his mate. But since she didn't know what was going on, she said goodbye to the pups, who seemed to know something was happening since they had quieted down, and then she nodded at Gwen before following Mitchell out of the yard.

Gideon and Brie whispered to one another as they walked ahead of them, while Dawn walked by Mitchell's side, confused as to why anyone would want her to meet this guest of theirs, but if she could help in any way, she would. It just didn't seem that likely.

"Can you tell me who it is?" Dawn asked softly. "Now that we aren't in front of others?"

Mitchell placed his hand on the small of her back, and she sucked in a breath. He kept casually touching her, and she couldn't keep her breaths steady when he did.

"It's Audrey. She's the Beta of the Aspens, and says she has something important to tell us."

Dawn stopped in her tracks, her eyes wide. "What? Why would Gideon want me there? I've never met the Aspens before, but I know they don't like us."

Mitchell moved so he stood in front of her. "Blade and a few of his people have issues with everyone. As for Audrey? I don't think she has issues with you or yours at all. I don't know her well enough yet, but I won't let her come near you or hurt you in any way."

Dawn wanted to feel a little ball of hope at those words but knew they only came from his dominance, not from caring. And she had to remind herself that she didn't *want* him in any way that was more than what they had—even if she didn't know what that was exactly.

"I wonder what she wants," Dawn said instead of responding to his words.

"I guess we'll find out, but if Gideon has a sense that something is important like this, then it's his wolf's instinct driving him."

Dawn thought of the ramifications of that statement and frowned before moving to the side so they could keep going. "Will Cole be able to do things like that?"

Mitchell put his hand back on the small of her back, and they continued their way to the front gate, their tempo a little faster since they'd stopped. She ignored the way the heat of his hand shocked her system.

"Yes," he answered, "Though it will take time. Gideon wasn't always the Alpha he is today. He's grown. The same way we all have. And you and Cole will, as well."

Before she could say anything to that, they were at the edge of the den and near the sentries. Gideon and Brie stood there along with Kameron and a tall blonde woman with light eyes and a lean, muscular body. Dawn didn't know who she was, but by the scent of her, she wasn't a Talon.

It must be Audrey, the Aspen Beta.

Yet...there was something *off* about her scent. Not
that she was an Aspen, Dawn had expected that, but
there was something...different.

"Alpha, thank you for meeting with me."

"Call me Gideon, Audrey. Have you met my mate,
Brie?"

"We haven't met," Brie said, holding out her hand.
Dawn should have been surprised that the submissive
wolf mated to the Alpha would be so forward with
touching another wolf even in a handshake, but she
wasn't. Brie was adept and knew when to hold back
and when to make the first move—something Dawn
needed to learn. "Nice to finally meet you."

Audrey looked taken aback for a moment before
reaching out to shake the other woman's hand. "You,
as well." She cleared her throat, glanced in Dawn's
direction before turning back to Gideon. Apparently,
the other woman knew who she was or didn't care
since they hadn't been introduced. "I need to tell you
something that might mean my death since it goes
against the rules of my Pack, but it's something you
need to know."

Dawn blinked, startled by Audrey's frank words.

"If it means your death and going against your
Pack, then why are you so willing to tell us?" Gideon
asked, his wolf near the surface but not in his tone. If
it weren't for the glow of his eyes, Dawn might not
have recognized his dominance with the way he held
himself back.

Audrey raised her chin and met Gideon's gaze for
a brief moment before lowering her eyes. If she could
do even that, then the woman must be far more
dominant that Dawn knew. There was a reason she
was the Beta of a large Pack of shifters, after all.

"As I said, there are things you need to know.
Things that Blade will use against you if he can."

"We're not at war with Blade," Gideon growled softly.

"No, but you and I both know that Blade isn't one to use something as trivial as peace to hold him back from getting what he wants."

Gideon stared at the woman for a moment more, and Mitchell leaned into Dawn's arm as if trying to soothe her wolf. Thankfully, everyone was focused on the others and not the two of them, or they would have easily seen what he did. Dawn wasn't even sure why he was trying to soothe her, or how she felt about it, but she knew this wasn't the time or place to deal with those things.

"Follow us to a place where we can talk in private, but know that if you even look like you're going to attack my mate or my people, I won't care that you're the Beta of the Aspens." Gideon's wolf was finally in his voice, and Dawn's wolf lowered its head in submission.

Audrey nodded and followed Gideon and Brie while Dawn and Mitchell brought up the rear. Mitchell once again put his hand on the small of her back, and she forced herself not to react. Once they were finished with whatever this was, the two of them needed to talk. She truly didn't understand his mixed signals, and they both deserved better than that.

Soon, she found herself in a small room, empty except for a lone table and a set of chairs. She wasn't sure what this place was used for, but she figured she shouldn't ask right then.

"What is it you need to tell us?" Gideon asked, his arms folded over his chest. Brie stood beside him though slightly behind. They moved as one, as if they knew their roles within their relationship and bonds deep down in their souls.

A small ache echoed within Dawn, and she wondered if it came from what she personally didn't have or the fact that she hadn't seen anything like that in most of her Pack. There were only a few mated pairs within the Centrals since many of the elders and young that left the old Pack weren't mated at the time, and without Pack bonds, there were no new mating bonds. One day, she hoped her people would have something like this, a Pack so healthy—even with its faults—that the Alpha and his mate could meet with a potential enemy and have no issues. Perhaps her brother would find his mate one day, and she'd watch him grow into his role with a woman by his side that centered him the way Brie seemed to do with Gideon.

Mitchell's fingers brushed along her arm, and she pulled herself out of her thoughts to focus on what was going on in front of her rather than what could be.

"It might be better if I showed you," Audrey said after a moment before letting out a breath. "Okay, so I didn't realize it would be this awkward, I mean, I *knew* it wouldn't be easy but..."

Dawn frowned and took a step toward the nervous woman before she'd even thought about it, her wolf needing to ease. Mitchell gripped her forearm, stopping her.

"What's wrong?" Brie asked softly. "You can just tell us what's on your mind, Audrey. Nothing should be so serious that it makes you feel this way."

Audrey ran her hand over her face, making her look much younger than she had before. "I'm sorry. I've never actually done this before, and it's hard to do something that's so against what's ingrained in me." The other woman blew out another breath and rolled her shoulders back. "You've probably noticed something different about my scent. There's a reason for that. I'm not a wolf."

Dawn froze, and she swore she could have heard a pin drop within the room—everyone was utterly silent.

"What are you saying?" Gideon asked. "Wolves were the only shifters in existence when the moon goddess changed the first hunter."

Audrey shook her head. "They were the only ones in *known* existence. Did you really think wolves were the only animal she changed? After all this time? Well, of course, you did. Because that's what we've led people to *believe*."

"Prove it," Mitchell said softly. "I knew something was off with your scent. So prove it. Then shift back and tell us what it means."

Audrey nodded. "I can tell you what it means right now. It means that Blade has kept this secret for years for reasons only he knows. Reasons I don't understand. But the man doesn't like change, and that means he's not ready for the society we're facing. He's becoming more and more aggressive. More and more secretive. I don't know what it means in the long run for any of us, but you need to be aware of things you don't know. Especially now. There are rogues on the loose, wolves still suddenly vanishing, and humans are still afraid of us. You and the Redwood Alpha seem to care. Blade does not. And that worries me."

And with that, she stripped out of her clothes and began to shift. If they'd been human, the sight of a woman stripping naked in front of a group of others might have been unusual, but they had been born into this world.

Only Dawn wasn't sure she knew what world this was anymore.

Especially when a large, golden lioness prowled out from behind the desk.

She heard Brie's intake of breath, and felt Mitchell's grip on her arm tighten. But all she could do was stare at the shifter before her, knowing everything had changed...and yet...she had no idea what might come next.

None of them did.

CHAPTER ELEVEN

Mitchell stared at the lioness in front of him and tried not to let the shock rocking his system show on his face. Considering he'd spent most of his life hiding his emotions from others, he hoped he was doing a decent job of it. Touching Dawn calmed him more than he thought possible, though, especially considering that every time he was near her, he was usually on the other end of serene.

"Oh my God," Brie muttered under her breath.

Dawn sucked in a breath beside him, and Mitchell couldn't help but agree with both of them. His amazement of the shifter in front of them was just as great.

Wolves weren't alone in this world.

And it sounded as if this wasn't a new thing.

Well...damn.

He hadn't been aware that he'd said that aloud until Kameron snorted beside him. He'd forgotten his cousin was even in the room, but considering his attention was on Dawn and the potential danger in front of them, he wasn't all that surprised. For such a dominant wolf, Kameron could hide in the shadows damn easily.

"Well, damn indeed," Gideon whispered, though since they were all shifters, it wasn't much of a whisper.

Audrey sat down and blinked up at them before opening her mouth wide in a yawn. If Mitchell hadn't scented the determined nervousness coming from her, he'd have thought she was bored. As if she showed off her cat self while alone in a room with an Alpha of a wolf Pack, his mate, two other dominants, and a maternal dominant that wanted to calm the jittery lion all the time.

A lion.

It seemed that no matter how long he lived, fate wanted to surprise him as much as possible.

"I have questions..." Gideon trailed off before shaking his head with a gruff laugh. "Lots of questions."

The lion gave them a nod before going back behind the desk, presumably to shift back.

"Will changing back and forth so quickly tire you?" Dawn asked, then seemed to regret her question. "Sorry," she said with a wince. "I just know I'd be exhausted. I'm nowhere near Audrey's strength, but I don't know if I'd be comfortable doing that alone in a Pack that isn't mine." She looked up at Mitchell. "Sort of how I am now...actually."

Audrey gave her a look before shaking her head and beginning her shift. Mitchell turned away since he knew shifting in front of others wasn't always the easiest thing to do—especially after doing it so close to another shift.

"Are we finishing our talk here?" he asked Gideon.

His Alpha shook his head. "Let's go next door." He kissed Brie's hair and ran his hand down her back. "It's a little more comfortable in there." He winked at Dawn, though Mitchell knew everyone was a little off-kilter.

"I'll get some food for all of us," Mitchell said next. He turned toward Audrey, who was almost done with her shift. "You'll need the energy I would assume, and we'll eat the same as you if you're worried about poison or something."

Kameron snorted again, and Mitchell held back a laugh. Apparently, one night with Dawn, and he was rambling as much as she did. Add in the fact that his whole world had just been rocked a few moments ago, and he was surprised he could even string two words together.

Cats.

There were shifter cats.

And one of them was the Beta of the freaking Aspen Pack.

The ramifications of what was just revealed hadn't even hit him yet, and all he could think about was the fact that Dawn stood right next to him, the softness of her skin brushing along his.

He knew it had been a mistake to give in to his attraction. Knew he'd make more mistakes with that one temptation. Yet he couldn't help himself. Not now...maybe not for a long time.

Dawn leaned into him for a moment before moving away and going to where Audrey had left her clothing. She and Brie gathered up everything and handed them over to the other woman, essentially blocking her from view. He liked how quickly Dawn went into maternal mode and worked alongside Brie. He wasn't even sure she realized she was doing it. Once the Centrals found their hierarchy, he knew

Dawn would flourish. What she needed was a *Pack*. And the fact that he was focusing on her and not on the thousand other things he should be concentrating on just told him he was off his normal path and he had to get his act together.

Soon, he found himself sitting next to Dawn as the rest of the Brentwoods filled the room, and everyone began to eat. Not all of the Brentwoods, though, Mitchell noticed. Max hadn't come, and neither had Ryder's mate, Leah. Mitchell understood that she had a sick baby at home. And, Max, according to Gideon, was with the elders. Mitchell only hoped that his brother was taking in all he could from Xavior and the others because he needed to find something to hope for.

Anything to cling to.

When they entered the room, Audrey had looked a bit nervous at first, but as Brie and Dawn talked to her, the Beta's shoulders relaxed. That was what the other two women were good at—putting others at ease—and Mitchell was grateful for it.

"Are there more of you?" Gideon asked, a frown on his face.

"I can't answer that," Audrey said simply before raising her hand. "I came here to tell you of my existence and the fact that I think Blade is either planning something or on the way to doing so." A pained look crossed her face, and Mitchell understood. She'd betrayed her Alpha to possibly protect her Pack. He'd have done it with his uncle if he'd been able to, but other events had forced him to hold back until the right time. "I can't believe I just said that aloud." Audrey stood up and began to pace. Her beast's agitation spoke to his own, and he knew it only served to increase the tension in the room, but

she needed to move around, and the Brentwoods
needed to let her.

"We're not going to tell Blade you mentioned it,"
Gideon said wryly. "And don't tell us any more if
you're going to break your bonds to your Pack in order
to do so. We'll figure it out."

Audrey let out a breath and looked around at the
room. "There are things I can't say. Things that aren't
mine to share. And I can't even tell you that I'll help
you more than revealing what I just did. I just..."
Audrey's eyes went gold for a moment before she
blanked her face. "The moon goddess spoke to me.
Told me I needed to do this. I don't know what it all
means, but I can't turn my back on her...even though I
feel like I just turned my back on my Alpha."

"Let's not go that far," Gideon said slowly. "Did he
order you not to tell us?"

Audrey shook her head. "It's understood."

"But not an order," Mitchell repeated. "You didn't
betray your Alpha. You listened to the moon goddess."

"Technicality." Audrey rubbed her fingers over
her temple. "I need to go. I have a meeting with my
elders soon, and I can't be late. I figured you should at
least know there are others in play." She turned to
Dawn and Mitchell. "Blade isn't happy with the
Centrals, even though your former Pack never hurt
him. So be on alert."

"Are you threatening the Centrals?" Mitchell
asked, his voice a growl.

"No." Audrey's eyes went cat. Well, hell, a *cat*.
That was something new he would have to work into
his thinking. "I'm saying Blade doesn't like change,
and things keep changing quickly."

Gideon and Kameron led Audrey out, continuing
their conversation, and most of the others started
their way out of the room, as well. He knew they

would talk about what they'd just learned and the possible ramifications, as well as the fact that every single one of his family had noticed the way he touched Dawn, but for now, he was alone with her as they walked back to her car. And he had no idea what to do.

"Were you expecting something like that?" Dawn asked, her voice a little breathy.

He looked down at her briefly before tearing his gaze away. "I don't think anyone expected something like that."

"But Gideon wanted me there..."

Mitchell frowned, nodding at one of his fellow Packmates as they passed, a curious look on his face when he looked at Dawn at Mitchell's side. There would be no hiding the rampant rumors after this, and yet Mitchell wasn't sure what he was going to do about that. It wasn't fair to Dawn, but he didn't know if he could walk away right then. He was a damn bastard through and through.

"Gideon might have wanted you there because you're a representative of the Centrals. I just don't know at the moment."

They reached the front entry, and Dawn paused, blowing out a soft breath. "I should go back to the den. I promised my mom I'd help with the rebuilding." She turned and looked up at him, and his wolf bucked, wanting to touch the softness of her skin even as it ached with the loss that would never go away.

"Be alert on the way home." If he'd been any other man, he'd have offered to drive her home, to make sure she was safe after Audrey's dire warning, but he wasn't that man. He needed to step away from Dawn, to breathe without her scent in the air because with each passing moment, the sense of betrayal coated his skin like sweat more and more.

Dawn was not his mate. He'd had his mate and lost her. He couldn't do this again. No matter how much he and his wolf fought both sides of the coin.

"You don't really think that Blade will come after me, do you? I know Audrey warned us about the unknown, but I don't think he's planning to come after a barista with no true Pack."

Mitchell held back a growl. "You were a *barista* when that rogue attacked you."

Dawn's eyes widened. "He wasn't Aspen, Mitchell. He was just a wolf that got too close to his animal. It happens. It's horrific, and I'm grateful you were there, but we have no evidence that it was Blade. And thinking that might enrage your wolf enough to where you'll make a mistake." She reached out and pressed her hand to his chest. "You have more to worry about than just me. You have an entire Pack that relies on you. Don't forget that."

"We don't know anything at this point, and you need to watch your back regardless." His phone buzzed in his pocket, and he cursed before taking it out and reading the screen. "I need to go."

"So do I." She licked her lips. "We need to talk eventually, Mitchell." The last part was a whisper. "We didn't get a chance to before."

He clenched his jaw and gave her a tight nod. "I agree."

She gave him a wobbly smile and stepped back. "Okay, then."

"Shit," he mumbled under his breath, at a loss for what to say or do next. Instead, he lowered his head and kissed her softly on the lips. His wolf immediately backed off, the contact just enough to soothe and entice at the same time. "I'll come to you tomorrow.

We'll talk." What he would say, he didn't know, but he knew that he couldn't stay away, even if that would be the best thing for both of them.

His heart had already chosen once and broke because of it. His soul was now a tattered remnant of what he knew he could never have again.

But he couldn't stay away from Dawn.

And that might just break them both in the end.

The next morning, he ran a towel over his wet head before chugging back the rest of his cooling coffee. He'd slept like hell again, and needed all the caffeine he could get. He stood in his bathroom, wearing only his jeans and a sleepy expression. His wolf was passed out, probably exhausted from pacing back and forth under Mitchell's skin all night. The damn thing hadn't let him sleep or keep his mind on the myriad of other things he should have been focusing on.

Instead, he'd only thought of Dawn and the fact that if she hadn't texted him when she got home, he'd have found himself at her door, needing to make sure she was safe.

I'm home.

Two little words had calmed his wolf when nothing else could—other than possibly hearing her voice.

He didn't understand why he was reacting this strongly, other than the fact that she was his potential mate. He shouldn't be feeling the mating urge like this, not when he'd done this before, but he was a damn shifter and didn't have a choice.

If he were any other man, he'd have been able to let go and drown in her scent. He'd be able to wrap her strength around him and learn the woman she was. He'd be able to fully appreciate her kindness and willingness to do anything for her family.

"Damn it," he growled under his breath, leaning forward so his hands gripped the edge of the sink. He had to get his wolf and needs under control. It wasn't easy, however, when his mind kept going in a thousand different directions and he couldn't make a damn decision.

"Mitchell?"

He stood straight at the sound of Walker's voice and cursed again. He was running pretty late if Walker was already in his house asking where he was. Usually, it was the other way around since his cousin was generally at the clinic or with another Packmate at all times. Mitchell was typically the one pulling the other man in the right direction.

"Back here," he called. "I'm almost ready." He splashed cold water on his face, dried off once again, and pulled on a cotton T-shirt that was beginning to get threadbare. He was just pulling on his shoes when Walker strolled into his bedroom, a brow raised.

"I don't know that I've ever seen you be late to anything," Walker said with false awe in his voice. "I should write this down somewhere, shouldn't I?" He held up his hands and smiled. "Or maybe you need a Healer? I mean, it's sort of what I do."

Walker flipped off his cousin, a smile playing on his lips. For so long, his family had been under so much pressure that they rarely made light of anything. Though it was still odd for Mitchell to not feel constantly on edge, he couldn't help but feel relieved that they could joke around—even poorly made jokes such as that one.

"I slept for shit," Mitchell grumbled. "Sorry I'm running behind."

Walker stuffed his hands into his jeans pockets and leaned against the open doorway. "No problem. We're just going for a run around the perimeter on the neutral zone side. It's not like we're on shift."

That much was true. Even though they weren't on sentry or watch duty, he and his family liked to make sure they were still seen out and about as a show of support to the rest of the Pack. He personally liked being in the loop with many of the different positions around the den since it made it easier for him to see what was lacking or what needed fine-tuning. Reports he received from others were invaluable, but seeing things with his own eyes made him a better Beta.

"Human form, right?" Mitchell asked, and Walker nodded when he glanced over. They did their runs together in either form depending on their mood. Today, however, Mitchell wanted to be able to talk to anyone who needed him since he knew the atmosphere around the den was a little anxious. Rumor had spread that Audrey had shown up at the den, as well as Dawn, but no one knew exactly why Audrey had been there. Dawn was easy since they knew she was training to be a true maternal female. Why the Beta of the Aspen Pack was there was harder to explain, especially since Gideon and the rest of them didn't want the secret that had been revealed yesterday out in the Pack.

Mitchell wasn't sure what Gideon or any of them was doing to do with this new information, but maybe on his run with Walker, he'd be able to order his thoughts better. Of course, with Dawn on his brain and her scent still in his system, he wasn't quite as sure about that as he probably should be.

Mitchell grabbed his phone and headed out of his bedroom, following Walker through his house. "Did you want coffee?" he asked.

"Already poured two travel cups for us," he said and gestured to the dining table. "They're from my place, not yours, so don't worry, you weren't *that* late."

Mitchell shook his head and picked them both up before handing one to Walker. He took a sip, the bitter brew sweetened slightly for him since they all knew their caffeine tastes, and headed out of the house on Walker's tail.

"So...cats," Walker said after a few minutes.

"Cats." Mitchell took another sip of his coffee and frowned. "Doesn't seem possible, and yet...it probably should have been on our radar this whole time, you know."

"I'm not sure I'd have believed her—odd scent and all—if you guys hadn't told me you saw it firsthand. But as for keeping it a secret from us for so long? I don't know that I'd blame anyone for that. We wolves—I guess I need to say *shifters* now—are a secretive bunch."

"Yeah, and Blade hated us even before the Unveiling. Thought we were too young to lead."

"As we're all over a century old, Blade is a dumbass."

"Truer words..." Mitchell grumbled. He was just about to say something else when a scent caught his attention on the wind, and his wolf went on alert.

"The hell?" Walker asked before the other man turned on his heel and ducked, his shoulder barreling into the side of a shifter in wolf form that had leapt at them. Their coffees hit the ground, forgotten.

"Walker!" Mitchell called out as he moved forward. His claws pierced the edge of his fingertips, and he slashed out at the wolf that jumped at his cousin again. Another wolf came out of the trees, and both Mitchell and Walker fought as a team against them. Like the rogue in the alley, he couldn't scent a Pack on them, but that didn't mean anything anymore, not with the way bonds and scents had shifted so much in the past few years.

From the rabid look in their eyes and the use of their fangs and claws with no provocation, all while on neutral land, these wolves were rogue, and that meant they wouldn't stop fighting until they gasped their last breath.

A *third* wolf came at them, and Mitchell sent a pulse through his bonds to his Pack, hoping Kameron or someone else would be able to feel it and come running. There wasn't another soldier on duty around this area since Mitchell and Walker had said they would both be there, and neither of them had time to call or text anyone for help.

The two of them could take out these wolves, but he didn't know if there were more, or if there were other attacks happening around the den. His wolf howled, needing to ensure that his people were safe. Fuck, he needed to make sure the other person who had been attacked recently was safe.

A burn crept over his back as claws sliced him, and he cursed, pissed off at himself for getting distracted at the worst possible time. He lashed out and got the wolf by the neck, slamming it to the ground. The wolf whimpered, and Mitchell did his best not to kill him since he didn't know exactly what was going on, but when he looked into its eyes, he knew it was too late. Grey had bled over its irises, and Mitchell knew the wolf was too far gone.

There was no coming back from that far over the brink.

With a prayer to the moon goddess for its soul, Mitchell snapped the wolf's neck quickly and as painlessly as he could. The wolf stopped moving, and

Mitchell let out a howl before turning and taking out the second wolf. Sorrow washed over him at the senseless loss. Walker finished with the third when Kameron shot through the trees at full speed, sweat covering his skin since his cousin wasn't wearing a shirt and only wore sweatpants.

"Talk to me," Kameron barked.

"Three rogues. No Pack scent." Just like before with Dawn, but this time, there were more wolves.

Walker pressed his hands to Mitchell's back, warmth spilling over him and pulsating along the Pack bonds as Gideon pulled up in a battered SUV. Mitchell knew Gideon was out of the den and over at the Redwoods today, so Gideon must have driven like crazy to get here that fast.

"Everyone okay?" Gideon growled out, his eyes gold. "What the fuck is going on?"

Mitchell told them what he knew as Walker finished up Healing the wound on Mitchell's back. "Thank you," he murmured, turning to get a good look at Walker. His cousin had a black eye, but nothing else that he could see. Since Healers couldn't Heal themselves, Mitchell was damn glad that Walker was okay. Usually, they didn't let the other man get too close to the fighting since, without Walker, they'd lose more wolves, and having a Healer was more important than having Walker fight by their sides. He knew his cousin sometimes resented it, but that was the way of Pack life.

However, even after all of this flowed through his mind, Mitchell's wolf knew he couldn't rest until he did one thing...

"I need to get to Dawn." Mitchell knew he sounded crazy, but he couldn't help the words pouring out. "I..."

144

Walker shook his head. "Go. But when you come back, talk to us, Mitchell. For the love of the goddess, talk to us. I don't know what's going on between you and her, but if you need us, we're here. All of us."

Gideon and Kameron gave him tight nods, and his Alpha threw the SUV keys at him.

Mitchell wasn't sure what to say, so he gave his cousin a tight nod, wiped his bloody hands on his jeans, and ran to where Gideon had parked the vehicle. He needed to see her, needed to know that she was okay after his own rogue attack. Two assaults so close together didn't make sense, and his wolf pushed at him to see her face, to scent her, and...even do the unthinkable and make her his.

He knew he was making a mistake, yet he couldn't stop running.

Not to her. Not to a future that could never be.

He just couldn't stop.

CHAPTER TWELVE

Dawn was out of the house before Mitchell had even pulled up. Walker had called ahead to make sure his cousin arrived safely and to warn them about the rogue attack. She hadn't been able to think clearly since. Her heartbeat was a rapid staccato in her ears as she ran down the stairs toward the sound of tires crunching on gravel.

Mitchell opened the door to his SUV right as she made it to his side, and she stopped suddenly, her wolf right under her skin, and her heart in her throat. She scented blood, and she wanted to find whoever had hurt him and kill them herself—though she knew he'd have taken care of them himself.

He slid out of the seat and ran his hands through her hair before crushing his mouth to hers. Startled for only a mere breath, she leaned into him, craving his taste and needing to make sure he was alive and safe.

He pulled away before she was ready and rested his forehead on hers. She could feel his wolf prowling beneath his skin, brushing up against hers, a savage and primal instinct that was beyond human, transcending desire.

They weren't two people standing in front of her empty house in a parking lot.

They were two wolves, two shifters connected to their animal selves that needed to make sure one another was safe. It didn't matter that they didn't know what any of this meant or that they'd made no promises to one another beyond that there would be no promises.

None of that mattered, because right then, they were shifters, not human.

"You smell like blood," she whispered, her voice hoarse.

Why did she feel like this? It didn't make any sense, and if she focused on it any more tonight, she'd hyperventilate.

"Walker was there," Mitchell whispered. "He Healed what he could, but I didn't check to see." He cursed under his breath and stepped away. Immediately, she felt the loss, but she ignored that and her wolf. "I didn't even wait to talk to Gideon or Kameron who were there to see what happened. I just *left*."

For her.

Or, at least, something to do with her.

She wouldn't let any guilt slide in, though. Not when she had nothing to do with his decision. He'd been the one drawn to her, just like she was to him.

"Call them," she said. "Call and get an update, but do it in the house so I can check you out and make sure you're not more hurt than you're letting on. Walker could have missed something."

Mitchell scowled at her, but she didn't lower her gaze. He might be more dominant than she was, but he was the one who came to her, had been the one to make love to her just a few days before, so he'd just have to deal with her meeting his eyes.

Her wolf dealt with it.

His wolf would have to, as well.

"Come on." She tugged at his hand, but he wouldn't budge. The man was like a wolf with a thorn in its paw. "My parents are out on patrol for the day, and my brother is staying with his friends in the city for the next couple of days on a break I forced him to take." Cole was actually staying with a woman and a man that she hoped might one day end up being his mates, but she didn't mention that. Maybe once she and Mitchell got to know one another better—if that ever actually happened—she'd tell him her wishes for Cole. Not now, though.

This man confused her to no end, but if she didn't get him inside and shirtless so she could get that blood off his skin, she was going to claw him herself.

Finally, Mitchell seemed to stop fighting himself and started moving. She didn't let go of his hand, though she knew she probably should, she just led him into her house. She'd left the front door open, so they walked right in where she'd been having her breakfast and going over the latest reports from around the den. She wasn't the Beta to the Pack, but she was Cole's sister and would do anything to alleviate some stress and help him have a life beyond what might be coming from the moon goddess.

She watched as Mitchell took note of her small but sturdy home and the remains of her breakfast on the kitchen table, but he didn't say anything. She tried to see what he saw but didn't find anything wrong with her home.

Her den hadn't always been here, so building permanent structures where they weren't hiding from wolves they weren't sure would ever accept them wasn't easy. But no matter how many times they moved from house to house, shed to shed as a kid, she'd had her family and the memories that came with them.

"You're still wearing that bloody shirt. Take if off."

"You just want me naked." He growled it out, though she wasn't sure if she caught heat in his words.

She raised a brow and reached for a kitchen towel so she could wet it down and clean him up. She wasn't sure he'd let her tend to him beyond that, but there was no way her wolf would allow her to do anything less.

"Shirt. Off. Now." This time, she growled it. "Call your Pack and figure out what you missed when you ran off. And let me freaking take care of any wounds you may have."

Wordlessly, Mitchell stripped off his shirt, and she did her best not to stare at the hard planes of his chest and those very sexy dips at his hips that she'd licked not that long ago. She'd only had a small window to learn his body, but she'd never forget the feeling of the scars beneath her hands when she kissed his chest.

Three long lines above his heart.

Ones she knew had to be more than just a battle scar for them to remain after all this time. But no matter how much she wanted to know about them, he'd have to be the one to tell her anything personal, and without her asking—she could never pull it from him.

"Walker took care of me." His jaw tightened before he visibly forced himself to chill out. "But I need you to stay close to me while my wolf relaxes. I need to know you're safe. And I have a feeling your wolf needs the same thing."

She swallowed hard, her wolf scraping along her skin as she met Mitchell's gaze. "What are we doing?" she whispered. It was the same question she'd asked him before, the one that was constantly on her mind.

He answered the same way he always did, the way she knew he'd answer. "I don't know, but I can't stay away."

"I don't want you to." She swallowed hard, wet the towel, and walked over to him, her heartbeat increasing as she moved closer. "Don't you need to call your Pack?" she asked, her voice barely above a whisper.

"Walker texted and told me I should stay here and make sure you're safe." His eyes glowed gold. "He's making that part up I think for my state of mind since the attack was only on that one part of the den and in a neutral zone at that."

Dawn wiped at the blood on his side, relieved to see that there were only slightly pink lines underneath, telling her they were freshly healed wounds rather than anything Walker might have missed.

"I texted my parents right before I heard you drive up." *And ran to him like you couldn't help yourself.* "They're all on alert just in case, but I didn't let Cole come back when I texted him. He needs the break."

"All Alphas—even potential ones do."

"I'm glad you came here." She held back a curse at that since she hadn't meant to say those words. "I don't know what will come of this, but I don't think I can stop wanting to be with you. And the fact that both of us needed to make sure the other was safe in a time of need and adrenaline? I think that even if we do nothing more than be with each other for the time being, we need to just *be* with each other."

Mitchell took the towel from her and set it down on the table next to them. "I can't be your mate, Dawn."

Something tore inside of her even though she completely agreed with him. "I can't be yours." Her voice sounded hollow yet laced with truth. "I don't want a mate, Mitchell. Not yet. Maybe not ever. I need to learn what Pack bonds feel like. I need to learn who I am beyond the daughter of the daughter of the daughter of a traitor. My family's legacy beyond these walls is a traitorous disgrace, and I need to know if I can live and breathe under that shadow with any semblance of grace."

Mitchell cupped her face. "You have more grace in your left pinky than many of the wolves I know, Dawn." Her heart broke once more. "I don't know if I can stay away. I can't fight this need. This pull."

"Then don't."

So when he finally, *finally*, leaned down and took her lips, she knew that she'd have him in her arms and know he was safe. She knew that once his scent mixed with hers once again, there was no going back, but no truly going forward either.

"I feel like I'm using you," he growled against her lips. "I'll hate myself more than I already do if I keep doing this."

She pinched his good side, and his eyes widened, his wolf at the surface. "I'm using you just as much as you're using me. So if we're going to do this, then we can be friends. Friends who have incredible sex and lean on each other if needed, just never with a bond." She kissed his lower lip, loving the way he growled and dug his hands into her hips. "Let our wolves do what they need to do. Just for now."

"Just for now." He kissed her harder, and she moaned.

Friends. She could do this. She *wanted* to do this. And when everything turned to hell later, she would remind herself of this feeling and the decisions she'd made for herself and what she wanted.

"Where's your bedroom?" he growled. "I thought about taking you right here on this table, but since it's your *family* table and anyone could walk right in...I'm just going to have to keep that for my fantasies."

She let her head fall back as he sucked on her neck. The damn man's voice could send her over the edge if she weren't careful. "Up the stairs, last one on the right." She squeezed her legs around his waist, bringing her core closer to his lower body. "Hurry."

He practically ran up the stairs, and she couldn't help the small smile that slipped out. His hand tightened on her butt, and he paused in the hallway after going upstairs to glower at her.

"Are you laughing at me?" He smacked her butt once, and she blinked, awed at the heat that shocked through her system.

"I wasn't—okay, maybe I was." She smiled widely, and he shook his head, a small smile playing on his lips. She never thought they'd smile when they did this. But they were supposed to be friends, and friends smiled and laughed with each other...right?

She raked her nails down his back so he would be able to feel them through his shirt, and he growled at her. She was careful not to touch him anywhere he'd been hurt during the attack, but she knew they *both* needed to feel.

When he reached her bedroom, he let her go, and she slid slowly down the front of him, making sure to touch every inch of him she could as she did so. His eyes darkened at that, and he lowered his head to kiss her, their tongues tangling, fighting for control.

When she pulled away and kissed down his chest before kneeling before him, he growled low and tugged on her hair. She shook her head and undid his pants, sliding them over his hips so she could reach under the waistband of his boxer briefs and grab hold of him.

He let out a strangled groan, and she finished undressing him just enough that his *very* erect cock was in her hand and right in front of her face.

"You took care of me last time. Now, it's my turn." And before he could say anything else, she slid her mouth over him and sucked. He let out a strangled moan before sliding his fingers through her hair and holding on, tight. And while he might think that gave him the control, she was the one with his balls in her hand and his cock in her mouth. She licked up the shaft and flicked her tongue along the opening on the tip before widening her lips and swallowing him whole again. He tasted salty yet just enough like Mitchell to make her wet. She moaned around him, increasing her speed and using her free hand on the rest of the length she couldn't fit inside her mouth.

When his balls tightened, and he let out a guttural groan, she increased her suction, then pulled back slightly so she could open her mouth wider. The first spurt hit her tongue, and she swallowed it up, taking the rest of him as he came in her mouth.

Before she could say something witty or charming, however, he pulled her up by her arms and crushed his mouth to hers. He'd kicked off his shoes and pants and had her on her back on the bed in the next minute. Using his claws, he tore off her clothes, and she couldn't help but be even more turned on. The damn man was hell on her wardrobe, but she didn't care right then. Mitchell past the brink and about to go down on her was the sexiest thing she'd ever seen in her life. She looked over him, taking in the long, lean lines of muscles that made up his chest and torso. Her gaze rested on his scars for a moment before going back to his eyes.

His jaw tensed just a brief second, but he relaxed so quickly, she wasn't sure she'd seen it at all.

Then he knelt on the floor at the edge of the bed, gripped her hips, and slid her right in front of his face. Before she could gasp, he had his mouth on her, and his fingers inside her pussy. He had one arm over her waist, keeping her down, and the other playing with her.

She arched, her body thrumming at his attention, then she gasped as he took *both* hands, pressed the backs of her thighs, and pushed her legs up so they were practically by her head. Then he licked, sucked, and nibbled on her until she was pretty sure she saw stars.

"Your cunt is so fucking sweet," he growled before going to town again. Seriously, if going down on a woman were an Olympic sport, this man would win the gold. Every. Single. Time.

She came in the next breath, her body shaking, and she tried to steady her rapidly beating heart as she heard the crinkle of a condom wrapper. She was so happy that he was thinking clearly since she wasn't. Neither one of them wanted to risk a bond—no matter what the quieter part of her whispered.

But before she could dwell on that, Mitchell had her ankles pressed together in one hand and his other hand on his cock.

"Ready?" he asked, his voice a growl.

She gripped the edge of the bed and nodded, needing him in her, *now*.

Then he thrust into her with one move of his hips, and she came again from that alone. He kept her legs pressed together so he made her squeeze him even tighter. She arched into him, their breathing syncing as he ramped up his thrusts.

And when he spread her legs again so he could lean over her, she sat up, wrapping her arms around his neck, and rocked her hips into him, meeting him move for move. Their gazes met as her nipples tightened and her body grew heavy. Instead of the glimpse of pain she'd seen before when she knew he was thinking of his past at the wrong instant, she saw only his feelings for her, however confused they may be.

And because of that, she kept her gaze locked with his, coming with him as their chests heaved and their bodies grew slick with sweat. He kissed her then, keeping her close even as her body slowly came down from its high.

"That was..." he trailed off, his voice hoarse. "You continually surprise me, Dawn, and I'm not surprised often."

She couldn't help but smile. "Well, old man, it's my job."

He grinned down at her, his chest still rising and falling quickly. "I could get used to this *friend* thing." He kissed her again. "But we'd better try it one more time. Just to be sure."

She wrapped her arms around him, totally on board with his plan. And if she kept telling herself that everything was okay, that they weren't making a huge mistake by ignoring the obvious, then one day, she might believe it.

One day.

CHAPTER THIRTEEN

Dawn's wolf itched beneath her skin, the coming moonlight almost burning across the paleness of her flesh. She stood shoulder-to-shoulder with Cole, staring up through the tall trees as she frowned. Sam stood on the other side of the porch, a frown on his face, as well. He wasn't as dominant as they were, so he had more trouble than most picking up scents and changes in the air. The fact that he felt anything then only told her that something was off tonight.

"There's something different in the air tonight."

Cole nudged her slightly. "You sound like a foreseer." Sam chuckled, his thin shoulders moving slightly and Dawn narrowed her eyes at her friend.

She tilted her head toward her brother and snorted. "Yes, Oh Wise One. I'm a foreseer. In fact, I've been hiding the secrets of the untold future from you all this time."

Her brother wrapped his arm around her shoulders and kissed the top of her head. "If that's the case, then I should beat you up for daring to keep things from your Alpha."

She pinched his side hard, and he yelped like he had when he was just a pup. "*Future* Alpha, Oh Wise One."

Sam laughed outright this time. "Can you tell me if you foresee me finding a mate who's stronger than I am? I think a nice dominant female would work quite nicely. What do you think?" He wiggled his brows, and Dawn smiled.

"That would be nice, right?" Of course, she wasn't just thinking of a strong female for Sam, but of someone she shouldn't want for herself.

Cole leaned over so his head rested on top of hers. She wasn't a small woman by any means, but her brother was a tall man with wide shoulders that she knew would one day allow him to stand proudly next to a man like Gideon and not look lacking.

Sam seemed to know that Cole needed to talk to her privately and said his goodbyes. She held him close for a moment, knowing that he was feeling just as out of place as she was at times. He didn't have many friends except for a wolf named Douglas and her. They were both a bit awkward in such an oddly fragmented Pack that was no Pack, and she knew that he was looking for something more like she was.

And though sometimes they both felt like outsiders, she knew he was as grateful for her as she was for him. Thankfully, though, she had her friends outside the den, but she wished Sam had more, as well.

Cole squeezed her shoulder, bringing her back to the present instead of twisted in her mind once more.

"It's coming, isn't it?" he asked softly, his voice that of her brother, not the man who would be her Alpha.

He didn't need to explain what he meant since the entire den had been feeling a sense of awareness all day. She wasn't sure exactly what would happen tonight—if it was going to happen at all—but her people hadn't gone too far from her home. Her parents were out with some of the elders, but they were still within hearing distance. Others mingled in the forest around the house, talking and drinking, needing to be close to one another with the sense of impending urgency in the air.

Right when she was about to ask her brother what the plan was, her wolf went on alert, and she almost dropped to her knees from the sheer force of awe and power slamming into her chest. Warmth spread through her limbs, and her blood pumped faster within her veins. Her wolf pushed at her, nudging at her, clawing until she knew that soon she would need to shift, but she held it back. She couldn't become her wolf until she knew the end of it and could make sure her Pack was safe. Others less dominant than she tore off their clothing as they began to shift.

Her brother gripped her shoulder tightly before letting go and throwing his head back. A howl ripped from his throat. Her voice joined his in perfect harmony, along with the voices of her people, her *Pack*, as they did the same and sang the music of their wolves, the song of their shifters long lost to the betrayal of others.

Something snapped hard inside of her, a long cord that connected her with those around her, tiny threads of varying sizes and strengths attached to every single person within her den. Another cord locked into place with her brother, a second to a man named Douglas, who had been born right before she and Cole.

As quickly as the magic had pumped into her, it faded away, and Dawn was left breathless, shaking, sweat-soaked...and Pack.

The Centrals had become a true Pack once again.

Her Brother was Alpha.

Douglas, it seemed, at least from what she could taste on the bond, was the Beta.

And she was...nothing.

Just Dawn.

She swallowed hard at that thought and looked at her brother, her eyes wide. "Cole," she breathed out. "Alpha."

She swore he glowed, though she knew that wasn't the case. But the sense of power wafting from him was new and yet controlled. Instinctively, she lowered her head, and out of the corner of her eye, she noticed the others doing the same. He wasn't their king, their tyrant; he was their Alpha, their ruler, their protector.

Warmth slid into her system and ran along the bond, a pulsating sense of power that told her that he would always be there for her, for their people.

Cole's arms slid around her and hugged her close. She wrapped herself around him and tightened her grip. "Thank you," he whispered, though she didn't know what for.

"You're going to be amazing," she whispered back. "And if you stray, I'll just kick your butt."

"Hence why I'm thanking you." He pulled back, and she met his gaze—though not for long since his wolf seemed extra dominant at the moment.

She winked and pulled away, trying to hide her disappointment. It wasn't like she'd thought she would ever be something more within the Pack, but she had thought *maybe* the moon goddess would have touched her, as well.

Soon, Cole was surrounded by the rest of the
Pack, forty others or so in human and wolf form
needing to touch their Alpha. Dawn stayed back
slightly to allow them the chance to find their peace
and settle down. If she was having a hard time
understanding what these Pack bonds meant and how
they would work, she could only imagine what the
others felt. Most of them had been part of a Pack once,
had felt the bonds sliding through their bodies and
souls before being agonizingly ripped from them.
Now, they were once again Pack, and she knew they
would need time to come to terms with that and
celebrate it, as well.

Sam stood by Douglas, his eyes wide as he met
hers. He put his hand on the back of Douglas's arm
and the bigger man relaxed marginally. She knew Sam
wasn't their Omega...at least not yet. But from the way
he comforted without thinking, the way he always
had, she thought perhaps he would be one day. He
was just dominant enough not to be a submissive with
similar powers.

Douglas looked shell-shocked, but Dawn couldn't
help but smile. He was a big man, who had been born
within the Centrals but hidden away as an infant. He
didn't remember the original den or what had
occurred all those years ago when their former Alpha
brought a demon to Earth to rain fire and hell down
upon them. He would be a good Beta, would care for
the others around him and learn how to help them
even when they didn't know they needed help.

From what she could tell, they didn't have an
Heir, Healer, Enforcer, or Omega, but that would
come. Either the moon goddess would bless others
within the Pack when they were ready, or babies and
matings would occur to bring them forth. They were

shifters, long-lived enough that not everything happened at once or even quickly.

Yet Dawn knew, no matter what happened next, she *knew* she would remain only Dawn: an unmated, maternal female with no title or children to help protect. And with that oddly depressing thought, she met her brother's gaze, and he frowned. She gestured toward her vehicle, and he gave her a nod, letting her know it was okay that she needed space at the moment. Others would be there to care for those who needed them, and they may even all shift to wolves and hunt. But for now, Dawn needed to get a grip on her emotions and figure out what was going on with her.

It wouldn't be fair to anyone for her to stay. She didn't want them to catch wind of her disappointment. She *shouldn't* be feeling this way at all, but she couldn't control her emotions, no matter how hard she tried.

Once she was sure the others weren't paying attention to her, she went into her house, slipped on her shoes, and grabbed her keys. She'd go for a drive and clear her head before she came back to celebrate. Her wolf needed time alone, and while she understood that, she also knew that if she weren't careful, she could hurt herself and others.

She wasn't even aware she was heading to the Talons until an hour later when she pulled up to the gate. The sentries nodded her inside even though she didn't have an invitation, and she was grateful that she didn't have to talk to anyone she didn't know and explain why she was there. Especially since she didn't know that either.

She parked in the visitor area and shut off the engine before resting her head on the steering wheel. Why was she there? It wasn't as if Mitchell was her mate and it would make sense for her to show up unannounced. Of course, they *were* friends, but they'd been very adamant about telling each other that they would be nothing more.

She ignored the niggling sense of doubt at her desire for that now that she knew what a Pack bond felt like. Because if the ties that connected her to those she loved were like this, she could only imagine what a mating bond felt like.

Dawn shouldn't be here. She should be with her Pack, celebrating and getting to know her people in a new light, learning the bonds and how they would work. Yet...she couldn't. There was something off, something that told her the others needed to celebrate but that she needed time apart.

And she hated herself for it.

A tap on the window startled her and told her she needed to get her head in the game because she should have damn well heard whoever it was come up, or at least *scented* them.

Mitchell frowned at her from the other side of the window, and she swallowed hard, trying not to let her wolf get too excited about seeing him. Darn it. She wasn't even sure what to do with these new Pack bonds inside her, there was no way she wanted a mating bond on top of that, and Mitchell wasn't the one to give her that anyway.

Yes, she *knew* they were potential mates. There was no hiding from that any longer, and they both understood that, but she'd just have to wait until she found another potential mate in the future.

Mitchell wasn't hers, and one day, she'd have to fully be okay with that.

He opened the door when she took too long to do it herself, and she undid her seatbelt. "What's wrong?" he asked, his voice holding the barest hint of a growl.

"Cole called almost an hour ago and told us you were heading over here after the moon goddess made you a full Pack. Why are you here, Dawn? Is something wrong? Are you hurt?" He reached inside and tugged her close so he could slide his hands down her arms as if checking for injuries.

"I'm fine," she whispered. *At least physically.* "Can I come to your place? I know I've never been there, but I don't want others to see me like this." A single tear slid down her cheek, and she knew she was just tired and overwhelmed. She was also in another Pack's den while she *should* be with her people. There was just so much emotion and confusion swirling inside her, she couldn't take it at the moment.

Mitchell nodded. "Of course. Come on, I'm not that far from here. Do you need to see Walker?"

She shook her head. "I'm not hurt. I...I shouldn't be here, but I couldn't stay there. Not right now." Plus, since Walker wasn't her Healer—and the Centrals still didn't have one it seemed—she wasn't sure what the other man could do for her other than witness her shame.

He took her hand, surprising them both, and led her past a few buildings and wolves on duty, who nodded at them as they passed. "Let's go, then." They walked in silence for a few more minutes, his hand over hers, the two of them catching the attention of others though Mitchell seemed to ignore it. Before long, she found herself in front a small cabin surrounded by trees. When he gestured for her to go inside after he used the security panel, she stepped into the entryway, and he closed the door behind them.

He cleared his throat, and she shifted from foot to foot. "I built this place with my brother when I became Beta and wanted a new start. Max lives just on the other side of the trees since we wanted to be close to one another." There was a sadness in his voice that pulled at her, but she wasn't sure what it was from. For Max, who had been injured in the last battle of the Unveiling, or for why they had wanted a new start to begin with.

"It's wonderful," she said after a moment, truly meaning it. The place had been decorated in masculine tones, but it wasn't too overt. Just enough so it looked as though a single man had lived there for a few years and made it his home. The entryway led into the living room with a dining room attached. Off to the side, she saw the opening to where his kitchen lay. Between the living room and the large table in his dining room was another archway where she assumed his bedrooms and bathrooms were. The placed seemed almost too large for one man—especially since she lived in a house only slightly bigger than this with her parents and Cole.

Mitchell cleared his throat, and she knew he was probably feeling as awkward as she was. Not so much because she was alone with him, but because she hadn't been with him in his place before. This was the second time in as many days that one of them had shown up at the other's in a time of need. If they weren't careful, they would indeed end up broken once this ended.

Of course, it would be her that lay in pieces.

She wasn't sure if Mitchell had ever been whole.

"Why don't we sit down, and you talk to me about what's going on in that head of yours."

She let out a breath and nodded before going to the large, L-shaped couch in the living room and sinking down into the cushions. "We're a Pack."

Mitchell nodded. "I know. Are you okay? I've never known anyone who was part of a Pack just forming, so I don't know what goes into it or how it feels."

She looked at him as he sat down next to her, not so close that they were touching, but close enough that she could feel the heat of his skin along hers. "It was odd. I had this feeling all day that something was...different, but it wasn't until the moon touched my skin that I knew that tonight would change everything. One minute, I was thinking about something—I don't remember what—and the next..." She shook her head, her voice trailing off. "The next... I can't explain it. But our Pack bonds snapped into place, as did Cole's Alpha and Douglas's Beta connections. I don't have words."

Mitchell tucked a piece of her hair behind her ear. "I know what you mean. I might have been born with my Pack bonds, but I wasn't born a Beta."

Dawn gave him a wobbly smile. "You get it then."

"What I don't get, though, is why you can't be with your Pack tonight. Was it just too much?"

She nodded, wiping a tear from her cheek before he could. She wasn't sure she could handle it if he kept touching her. "That and...it's going to sound silly and selfish if I say it out loud."

Mitchell shook his head. "You're talking to the bastard Beta of the Talon Pack, the most selfish one of them all, I'm not going to judge you."

She wasn't sure if he deserved that title, not if he was hiding his pain so much from others, but she didn't comment on that. "I've spent my life trying to grow up in a Pack that wasn't a Pack, knowing that one day we might be something more, that we might get more than we ever thought possible despite what happened in the past. I spent that time trying to find out who I was. Was I a maternal female? Yes, but I didn't know what that meant or what I could do about it because there was no one to nurture, no one to protect. Was I just a barista? Just someone who went along day to day and lived within the world, lived among the people who didn't truly know me, yet never once allowing myself to stand out or blend in. Just *being*. I've been trying to find out who I am, but at the same time, I knew I was waiting to see who I could be. And when the Pack bonds came, and I felt the Alpha and Beta bonds extend to the two around me...people who weren't me, I found out that everything I hadn't realized I'd been hoping and searching for was for nothing. *I* was nothing. And I know that sounds stupid and not completely true, yet I can't help but feel that way. I never thought I would be the Heir, or the Omega, or anything like that, not truly. But, apparently, some part of me, some part of my wolf at least, agreed with the others who said I was well suited for it and could help the Pack. They were wrong, and the part of me I hadn't known existed was wrong, too."

She closed her mouth, her cheeks pinking. She hated when she rambled like that, but she couldn't help it when she had so much on her mind and had been keeping everything inside for so long. Before she could say anything else, though, Mitchell lifted her up and set her on his lap. She was stunned at the way he held her, knowing he wasn't the most emotive person.

"You're not nothing, Dawn. You could never be *nothing*. First, you don't know what will happen in the coming days or months. For all we know, the moon goddess wanted to do things slowly and didn't want to overwhelm everyone right out of the gate. It's not like we know what she's thinking. She's a spiritual entity that, if I'm honest, scares me a bit. She's so unknown, and I hate the unknown. Secondly, even if you aren't part of the hierarchy, that doesn't mean you're not a valuable member of the Pack. A *needed* member. We have over three hundred wolves within our den alone, and many others outside the wards. Only a few of us have any *special* powers or connections, but every single member of the Talons is needed in some way."

Dawn leaned into Mitchell's shoulder and sighed. "I *know* that. I'm not jealous of Douglas, believe me. I didn't even want a position like that. I don't think I'd be ready for it. But I think I was on pause for so long because I didn't know what I *could* be that I didn't stop to think about what I already am, or what I could be for myself. I just kept saying that I needed to find out who I was, but I don't think I ever looked."

"I don't think that's true. I think you're constantly looking but also living at the same time. You're so fucking strong, Dawn. You care about your family and friends and do everything you can to protect them, even from what you perceive as your own weaknesses. You're not nothing, you're far from that. And once you realize that, I think you'll be an even stronger leader within your Pack and for yourself." He paused, but she didn't say anything. There wasn't much for her to say after that.

But in his arms, she thought that, just maybe, she could believe in something more than herself. But as soon as she thought that, she pushed it away, knowing she couldn't be that stupid. It would only lead to pain if she tried.

CHAPTER FOURTEEN

Mitchell held Dawn close, his wolf content for the first time in far too long, and he hated himself for it. No, he couldn't quite say that anymore. Only part of him hated the feeling that washed over him at the feeling of Dawn against him. But the rest? The rest knew that this could be his future if he only gave it a chance. But there was no way he could do that, no way he could let the woman in his arms feel anything less than cherished and centered.

So he had to walk away.

Eventually.

"Your Pack will grow," he said softly, pushing thoughts of what he shouldn't be thinking of out of his mind. "And you will grow with it." He ran his hand through her hair while trying to come up with what he was going to say next. "You see the Talons as they are now, but we weren't always this way."

"You were never a disgraced Pack like us, but yes, I know the Talons weren't always as...strong as you are now."

Mitchell snorted despite himself. "Hell, you aren't wrong about that, but in some ways, we were punished, as well. Our old Alpha, Gideon and the others' father, was an asshole. My and Max's father was an old fucker, as well, but Gideon's dad? He was a sadist who liked power but didn't know that he needed to take care of his people in order to *use* that power. He beat the shit out of his kids, verbally abused them, and killed whoever was in his way. His brothers, my dad and other uncles, weren't any better. Some of them might have even been worse if they were stronger. And our Pack wasn't able to do anything about it. We were worse than the Aspens with how insular we were, and because of that, there was no one to ask for help. And us kids didn't realize we could do anything about it until we were so weak, we almost died along with anyone else who didn't fall in line. We weakened the Pack bonds and lost many of our members like Parker, my cousin's mate, and Parker's mom and uncle. They're Redwoods now, though Parker is a Talon again since he mated Brandon and Avery."

Mitchell shook his head, his memories drenched in sorrow. "Slowly but surely, our connection to the moon goddess shriveled up. She didn't speak to us, didn't aid our Alpha or elders. And once Gideon became Alpha, it took *fifteen years* for her to bless us again with mating bonds and children. It's taken a long time, and we look normal again from the outside, but with our memories and our past, we are anything but normal. I'm just thankful for what we have, though I hope to the goddess that none of us forget what we lost along the way."

"I want my Pack to have what you have now. A future."

"You do. And the Talons and Redwoods stand by you." He didn't mention the Aspens. There was no need to since they both knew the score.

They were both silent for a bit longer, their heartbeats loud in the stillness of the room.

"You know," he said after a moment, not aware that he was going to say anything at all, "Between what I just told you and the three years we've been fighting the humans...it's odd to think now that we're in a time of peace." Ignoring the rogue attacks recently, there really wasn't an enemy to fight other than time. "I'm an old wolf," he murmured. "An old wolf without a war to fight."

Dawn turned in his lap then and faced him slightly. "Then don't fight. Live. Because no matter what happens, your Pack needs you."

He frowned, his wolf waking up slightly at her words. "And your Pack needs you."

"I never knew Pack bonds would feel like this. I mean, I'd heard about them and read what they were, but knowing what they feel like inside me is so different than what I thought. My parents are mates, I know that, but I don't know if they were truly able to feel their mating bond outside a Pack, not with everything coming down on them. I'm so happy they'll be able to dig into it again, and one day, the rest of the Pack can mate, too. The more bonds, the more relationships and connections, the stronger we'll be. Maybe never as strong as the Talons and Redwoods, but *whole*."

As soon as she mentioned mating bonds, he stiffened. He *knew* she'd said she didn't want one, but one day she would. One day, when she felt as though she'd found her place, she would want a bond. She deserved one.

And he would never be able to give it to her.

His wolf whimpered, and she cupped his face. He sighed, knowing he needed to tell her everything. It wasn't fair to keep pushing her away and holding himself back without the truth out there in the open. Only he'd never told a soul what he was about to tell her, and frankly, he wasn't even sure how he would go about it.

"There's something I need to tell you."

She looked up at him, and without speaking, moved off his lap so she faced him with her legs crossed in front of her. "What is it?"

His wolf let out a pained howl, but Mitchell knew if he weren't careful, he'd betray Heather and fall for the woman in front of him. Fall for her strength, her power, her grace. And no matter what, he couldn't break the promise he'd made to a woman who buried herself in his soul and memories forever ago.

For all the thoughts going through his mind and the years he had behind him, he didn't know how to tell Dawn what kept him up long into the night or what lay in the scars along his skin and soul.

"Thirty-three years ago, the only other person who knew what I'm about to tell you died by my hand," Mitchell began. Dawn reached out and gripped his palm, cementing him to the here and now, even though his memories were so far away he wasn't sure he could hold onto them for longer than a bare instant.

"My uncles were ruthless bastards, and my father, Abraham, the former Enforcer, was no better. He ruled his tiny corner of the Pack and those he lied to in order to protect the den. Or at least that's what he told us. Max and I took down our father when he tried to kill Gideon after the challenge that brought in our new bonds and Alpha. When the hierarchy bonds were stripped from them after our former Alpha died, the uncles and my father were already weakened, but they wanted to kill us all for daring to do the right thing and protect our Pack."

He let out a breath and ran his thumb along the fleshy part of her hand between her thumb and forefinger.

"He knew, though...he knew my secret because I couldn't hide it from him. Somehow, I hid it from everyone else, even our Alpha." He paused for so long that Dawn squeezed his hand.

"You don't have to keep going if it's too much. I get it, baby. Don't hurt yourself unnecessarily."

He shook his head. "But it *is* necessary. You're important. You're..." He couldn't finish that thought, and didn't know what he'd have said if he could. "You need to know, and I need to tell you."

"Then tell me. I'm here, Mitchell. I won't judge."

That wasn't what he was worried about. "Three years before everything came to a head, I found my mate."

Her eyes widened fractionally, but she nodded. "I had a feeling." Her voice was a bare whisper.

"Her name was Heather. She was a human who I met at the library of all places." He shook his head. The awed joy he'd felt at seeing her for the first time mixed with old pain and betrayal and tugged at the empty place where his bond used to pulse. "We were mated only a year before everything went to hell, but she was mine."

"But how did she hide from the Alpha? I thought once a human mated a wolf, she was part of the Pack."

"That should have been the case, but the Talons were already broken by that time. She never became a Talon, and there were no more matings after mine. My father only knew because he scented her and followed me to the house I shared with her one day."

He swallowed hard but didn't let go of Dawn's hand, wasn't sure if he could. "She never liked my wolf. I know the moon goddess doesn't make mistakes with matings, and I will never think of Heather as a mistake, but she never liked that part of me. I know it scared her, and maybe over time if I didn't have to hide her from my family—*all* of my family—in case someone accidentally slipped or was punished because of what they knew, something might have changed. But she never met Max. Never met my cousins. She only knew that she needed to keep who I was and who *we* were a secret or she could be in danger. No wonder she never wanted to see my wolf, never wanted to hear me growl or be anything more than human."

Dawn squeezed his hand again, and once more, he found himself centered enough that he could continue.

"One evening, she was on her way home from work and hit a bad storm. She went around a curve too fast and ended up slamming into a tree." Bile filled his throat at the memory, and he wiped his free hand over his jeans to dry the cold sweat that had broken out. "I felt her pain across the bond, and it shattered part of me. I don't think I ever ran as quickly as I did that night on my way to her. But I was too late." His body shuddered, but he needed to continue. "She died in my arms, even though I could have saved her."

Dawn frowned. "How could you have saved her? She was human, Mitchell."

His wolf growled. "I could have changed her. I was strong enough then, even though my father tried to beat that out of me. But Heather never wanted to change. She wanted to remain human throughout our mating."

Dawn's eyes widened as she seemed to understand what he was wasn't saying. "But...she would have gotten older eventually."

He nodded. "She'd have died an old woman, and I'd have stayed the same age I am now. At least, physically. I'd have watched her die in my arms at some point later, rather than bleeding out on the darkened, wet road. She never accepted me, and she never would have accepted her new nature if I'd changed her to save her life."

There were so many what-ifs, but he couldn't get into them. He'd had thirty years to ask what if.

Before she could speak, he continued, knowing he needed to or he wouldn't. "Losing her almost killed me." He used his free hand and softly scraped his fingers along his chest over the claw marks that lay there and would remain on his skin until the end of his days. "The bond broke, taking part of my soul with it. I can still feel the empty part of me where she used to be. She might not have known my wolf, but that was my fault. If I had been able to show her what our wolves *could* be rather than what she feared, she might have been able to stay with me—car accident or not. But when she left, she took part of me with her." He paused. "And, sometimes, it feels like everything."

Without words, Dawn scooted closer and wrapped her arms around him. He held her close, inhaling her scent. He'd thought that would make him hurt, but somehow, it reassured him.

There was no denying who she was now, though he wasn't sure there was ever a moment where he wasn't thinking who she could be. That was why he'd concealed himself from her, why he'd hidden from himself.

Dawn was his potential mate.

But he couldn't mate with her.

If he mated with her, he'd break again. He'd lose part of himself, betray Heather, and end up hurting Dawn in the process. Because no matter how many times he told himself that this was all about him, it wasn't.

This was about her. If he mated with Dawn, made a new bond where his old one had used to be, she'd know. She'd sense somehow that he hadn't always been hers alone. She deserved a whole man. A man who could love her with every part of himself, who hadn't been broken into so many pieces he wasn't sure how he came back together.

"I'm so sorry," she whispered.

He held her close, not sure what else to say. He missed Heather every damn day. She might have been scared of his wolf, but it hadn't been her fault. He'd known that then, and he surely knew it now. They could have had something entirely different, something healthy and whole if his Pack hadn't been on the verge of implosion and self-destruction.

"I understand why you told me," Dawn said softly. "Before you even said anything, I never would have begged for a mating bond, never would have felt as though we were lacking. Because no matter what, it's our choice." She turned so she could look him in the eyes, and his wolf brushed along his skin, needing to be close to her. "It still is." She licked her lips, and he shuddered out a breath, the weight of countless years of secrets and regret making him weary.

"Dawn..."

"Don't. Don't push me away. I came here because I needed to be held, and you're holding me just as I'm holding you. What we said before doesn't change. We might have had a chance at a mating if it was another time or we were different people. But..." She shook her head before meeting his gaze once again, this time a solemn determination in her eyes. "I'm not ready for that connection, and if and when I am, I need to be with someone who can give me everything. I won't ask you to be that man, and you don't need to *be* that man. But I think we were put together here, at this time, for a reason. And I...I'm not ready to walk away."

He leaned forward and kissed her lips softly. "I'm not ready either." But he couldn't stay forever. It wasn't fair to her, not when he had nothing left to give.

They held each other for a bit longer, and he hoped that she got whatever she needed from him. She'd been so *off* when she showed up, newly bonded to her Pack and feeling slightly disappointed. He didn't understand the reasoning behind the moon goddess's decision to keep Dawn out of the hierarchy—at least for now—but he hoped that Dawn would be able to learn what her purpose was in an ever-changing den.

Once they were both a little calmer, Dawn headed back to her place. He'd known she would have to eventually since she needed to celebrate with her new Pack, but he was oddly...honored that she came to him when she hadn't known what she was feeling. After all, he'd done the same with her just the day before.

Mitchell sighed as he watched her drive away. They were making a mistake relying on each other like this, teasing their wolves with a promise of eternity when there was no forever left to give.

But he couldn't walk away.

She couldn't walk away.

And when they both broke in the end, he just hoped there was someone that she could rely on to pick up the pieces. He'd said more than he'd ever said to another about Heather, but Dawn wasn't the only person he needed to tell. With a sigh, he turned and made his way to his brother's home.

Max needed to know, and Mitchell needed to tell those who'd been with him his entire life why he kept his secrets.

He just hoped they could forgive him.

And that one day, when things fell apart around him once again, they'd help him figure out how to live without his soul.

"Why did you need to see us?" Gideon asked once everyone had gathered in Mitchell's living room. They normally didn't meet there, in fact, he wasn't sure they'd *ever* had a meeting there, but he needed to be in his home for this. He wasn't sure he could have told them what happened if he'd been anywhere else.

Gideon sat on the couch with Brie by his side. Brynn and Finn had come from their home in the Redwood den since Mitchell wanted his cousin there, and Finn was family now even if he wasn't Pack. Ryder and Leah took seats on the floor next to Kameron, while Walker stood near the doorway with Charlotte, Bram, and Shane. The latter trio wasn't Brentwoods, but they were part their inner circle. Max stood by himself on the other side of the room, though Parker, Brandon, and Avery were seated near him at the long table that rarely had any use except to hold paperwork.

He wasn't sure he'd ever had this many people in his house before, and his wolf wasn't sure he liked it. But this was his family, his circle, and he had been lying to them long enough.

"Is it about Dawn?" Brandon asked. As the Omega, the other man probably knew more about what Mitchell felt than anyone, but he'd hidden so much from them.

"Almost," Mitchell said. He let out a breath and looked up into the faces of those that cared for him. He never should have kept Heather from them, but it hadn't been because of them that he'd hidden her. He'd tried to protect most of them from the former Alpha and the rest of that particular hierarchy, and in doing so, he'd kept his secrets so long that he wasn't sure how he should begin today.

So, instead of agonizing any more than he already had, he told them about Heather. Spoke of his father, and his reasons behind the secrets. Told them about the accident and how she hadn't been changed.

He told them how he'd lost part of himself and knew he wouldn't be whole again.

He didn't speak of Dawn, but her presence was felt nonetheless.

And when some of his family cried, the others held him or yelled—not at him, but at the fates that had tried to destroy their family once again, he knew that he'd taken one step closer to healing.

He just didn't know what he would do with that new scar on his heart. Dawn deserved far better than him, and yet he couldn't let go.

And now that he'd talked it over with his family, there was a small part of him growing in size with each passing moment that told him he might not let her go. Ever.

Betrayal coated him like it had before, but this time, it didn't stay quite as long, didn't feel quite as suffocating.

What did that mean? He didn't know, but he knew he needed to keep Dawn safe. Safe from the rogue that had wanted to take her out, safe from the

Aspens that might want to prove something and make a move against the Centrals...

And finally, safe from him.

EMBERS

"**N**othing is going as I planned," Blade growled low. "But then again, I didn't send out the best of my collection."

Blade had been keeping wolves from various Packs that had dared to come through his lands over the years. He wasn't like the humans who thought they knew best and performed tests, cutting open shifters just to see if their blood still ran red. He only kept them locked up, near starving, and slowly but surely severed their bonds to their Packs. That was, if they even had them. Some were lone wolves with no ties to others and no family to come after them to begin with.

Parker had been one of the only wolves he'd let off his land, that damn Redwood-now-Talon wolf had been far too visible and connected to too many for Blade to do what he normally did.

And that was to show *all* shifters under his "care" that he was the most dominant, most powerful wolf. He was the Alpha of all Alphas and should be recognized as such. Or at least, that was what he called himself. He growled. The Aspens were one of the strongest Packs in the world, if not the strongest ever. And once the world realized that, he would have that title in truth.

One day, when the time was right, he'd show the rest of his Pack and the rest of the *world* his power, and they would bow before him.

He growled, his claws tearing through his fingertips. Just thinking of other Packs made him want to gouge something. He still couldn't quite believe that the moon goddess had given the Central Pack their powers back. That fucking abomination of a group of wolves now had a fucking Alpha and a Beta and would probably have more in their hierarchy soon. And if they were left unchecked, they would bring another demon into the world and fuck up everything.

The Centrals were everything that was wrong with the world of shifters. The Centrals being allowed to live in relative peace was evidence that the Packs weren't taking care of their own. They weren't taking out the ones that proved themselves to be damaged. They were no longer keeping their wolves a secret and ensuring that they were the elite species.

Hell, these wolves were so mundane, they didn't even know the existence of *other* shifters. Only Blade knew that. He was the only Alpha who had more than wolves in his Pack. That clearly meant he was the more evolved and the one to rule all the Packs.

If only the others would get in line.

Once Blade was done with the Centrals, and then the Talons—and even the Redwoods—they would all bow before him.

As was his due.

"You're growling over there with a manic expression on your face. It's a little dramatic, don't you think?"

Blade turned at the sound of Scarlett's voice and frowned. "What are you doing here?" He hadn't scented her come into his bunker office, but then again, Scarlett was a powerful fire witch, part of the Aspen Pack, and could hide her scent if she so chose. She didn't always since not all of the Aspens knew of her power, but she liked to sneak up on some of them and learn their secrets. He was *not* pleased that she was doing it with him.

"You asked me to come, remember, your Alphaness?" The statuesque redhead rolled her eyes, leaning against the open stone doorway. She made a motion as if to buff her nails, and tiny flames danced along her fingertips.

"That fucking Beta killed three of my rogues and wasn't even badly hurt in the process."

"Well, you *did* send the wolves far too close to Talon territory, if you don't mind me saying."

He did, but since he needed her help just then, he didn't say so. Scarlett was testy on a good day, and he wasn't in the mood for her theatrics.

"I needed him out if I want to get to Dawn."

"And why is this one little wolf so important to you?" Scarlett prowled toward him, and he sighed. She moved more like a cat than a human witch, but since she was mated to one of his soldiers who *was* a cat, she must have picked up some of her mate's tendencies through the years they'd been together. Hence why Scarlett hadn't aged a day since she formed her bond. Her magic had only grown, as well. "She's awfully young for you, don't you think?"

Blade let out a growl, his wolf rising to the surface, and Scarlett dutifully lowered her gaze. "She's the sister of that damned fake Alpha and spending far too much time with the Talon Beta. There's not a bond there, but they have something going on, something

CARRIE ANN RYAN

that can only strengthen the Central and Talon treaty. We can't let that continue."

Scarlett nodded; flames dancing along her hands again. "And what do you need me to do?"

Blade let his wolf rise fully, his eyesight shifting ever so slightly, telling him he was seeing through the gold rather than his human eyes.

"Distract those who would protect her. My men will get the girl and bring her to me. Once I have her, I'll make her one of my pets...much like the others."

As if knowing they were being spoken of, the wolves he'd captured let out pained whines. *Damn shifters*, he thought, they never should have come to him for help or a place to stay. He hadn't been placed on this earth for charity. The moon goddess had given him a far greater purpose.

"I can do that." She paused. "You'd better watch out for Audrey," Scarlett said casually. "She's sniffing around again."

His Beta was getting far too curious for her own good. Too bad he couldn't take her out like he had her predecessor. There were, sadly, only so many *accidental* deaths he could cover up. As it was, he already had to keep an eye on his son and Heir since the boy wasn't shaping up how Blade wanted him to.

He sighed. Pack politics took far too much energy, especially when others didn't cower before him.

But they would.

Soon.

They'd tremble before they bowed and recognized him as what he truly was.

Their savior.

183

CHAPTER FIFTEEN

D awn leaned into Cole's shoulder and sighed. "Did you sleep at all last night?" "A little," he answered softly. "I'm a little energized, though, like my wolf got a boost when the bonds hit."

They stood on their porch like they were before when the Pack became whole, and she couldn't help but stretch, soaking in the power that radiated off her brother's skin. He was a force to be reckoned with. A protector. An Alpha.

He cleared his throat, and she looked up at him. "What?"

"Do you want to talk about where you went last night?"

She blew out a breath. "Not really. Plus, if you have to ask, then you already know."

"You smell like him, Dawn. Not just in a way that says you've been near him once in a while..." He paused as if trying to come up with what he was trying to say. "You're different around him. Altered when you come home from being with him. Not in a bad way, but...I don't know. It's like you're more settled and yet *not* at the same time." He shook his head and pulled away from her so they could see eye-to-eye. "He's so dominant, Dawn. Not just in his wolf, but also in the way he holds himself. I'm not going to lie, he intimidated me when we first met, and he started training us. He holds himself back and seems...almost dark. I never would have thought he'd be the one for you."

Dawn gripped the railing and looked off into the forest, knowing some of her Pack was out there running in wolf form after their hard run the night before and not wanting to go back to human just yet.

"He's not mine," she said firmly. And though she kept telling herself that was okay, that she didn't need to be with him, she knew that wasn't exactly the case anymore. The more time she spent time with him and the more she felt the bonds that connected her to her Pack, the more she knew she'd been lying to herself from day one.

Mitchell could have been her mate in another life, yet she wanted that bond in this one. Wanted the man she'd learned he hid beneath the hard shell that he'd made for himself as a result of his countless trials and tribulations.

"Dawn..."

She shook her head but couldn't look at Cole. "He's not mine," she repeated. "He's not my mate."

"Are you sure? Because Walker told us that the mating bonds are changing; they're not the same as they were before. It could be that your wolves just don't recognize what is what yet. It could take time."

"No, that's not it," she said quietly. "We're potentials. We've known for longer than we allowed ourselves to see. But in the end, we won't be mates."

Cole let out a low growl and reached for her hand. She pulled away before he could touch her, but that only made him growl louder.

"Has he hurt you? Who the fuck does he think he is to not want you as his mate? He'd be damn lucky to have you in his life? If he's fucking using you, I'll end him."

Goddess help her when it came to dominant males.

"First, if any man hurt me in that way, I'd be the one to handle it. Not you. You might be my big brother and now my Alpha, but I don't need you to beat up any guy in my life. I'm strong enough. Secondly, he's not using me." She swallowed hard. "If anything, we're using each other. Both of us knew going in that we weren't going to complete the mating bond even though we wanted to be near each other for the time being. Thirdly, we each have our reasons, and I'm not going to share those with you because they are personal, but know that it's not just him."

It wasn't, she reminded herself. It didn't matter that her feelings were changing, and she knew she'd hurt so bad in the end that she'd find it hard to breathe, but it wasn't Mitchell's fault. He had gone through hell and back, and sometimes, there was no way to heal those kinds of wounds.

"I still want to hurt him."

"Why? Because I'm having a sexual relationship with a man that I chose, knowing there is no future? A future I, myself, don't want?"

"Because I don't want my baby sister hurt." He pulled her into his arms before she could push him away and hugged her close. "I'll never stop you from doing what you need to do, but I'll always be here for you." He kissed the top of her head, and her wolf brushed along her skin, finally relaxing after a long night of tossing and turning.

"I love you," she whispered.

"Love you, too, Dawn. Love you, too." His wolf's presence wrapped around hers, and she let out a slow breath, settling slightly. She was far too confused and on edge to be truly settled, but at least she could breathe again.

After a few minutes of peaceful silence, Douglas came over to speak with Cole. Since everything was all still so new and they were still learning how their Pack would function, Dawn left them alone to, presumably, talk about den business. One day, there would be more people in their meeting, such as an Heir that would help lift the coming burden from her brother's shoulders. For now, though, the elders who had protected her as a child and had saved them all would be there to aid Cole when he needed advice and to help with their growing and evolving den.

As for Dawn...well...she'd be there for him, too. She was still Pack, even if her wolf felt pulled in another direction for some reason. And Cole was still her big brother. She'd do anything she could for him— except stay away from the wolf who could tear her soul apart.

Later that evening, Dawn found herself being led through the Talon gate once again. Brie had texted earlier and asked if she wanted to come by just to talk and play with the baby, and Dawn had said she would be there. When Dawn texted Mitchell to let him know she'd be at the den, he'd told her he would meet her at the Alpha's home.

She still wasn't sure what they were to each other beyond a potential disaster, but she wasn't going to waste any more time second-guessing her choices. She wanted this time with him, her wolf *needed* it. And if it weren't for the fact that she understood why he couldn't give her more than what they had, she might have been left wanting.

She pressed her forehead to her steering wheel after she parked and let out a sigh. She kept spinning herself in circles when it came to her place in her Pack, and now her place with Mitchell. She hated that others' fates made her continuously doubt her own choices in life. Once her wolf came to terms with the moon goddess's decisions, she'd be able to get over herself and do what she always did in the Pack— anything she could to help others. And when she finally got it through her skull that yes, she *wanted* that bond with Mitchell and got over it, she'd be happier. She'd been naïve to think she wouldn't want the mating bond once she found her link to her Pack. She honestly hadn't known what it would be like to even have one bond, let alone another that connected her to a wolf so intimately that she'd never be able to put a name to the sensation. But Mitchell couldn't have that, and she'd gone into their relationship thinking the same of herself.

Any pain she felt would be on her and her alone.

He hadn't changed the rules.

Her heart had.

"Damn it," she muttered. "Stop agonizing." With a determined grace, she slid out of her car and headed to Gideon and Brie's. She waved at some of the wolves she passed who smiled at her. She *knew* they scented Mitchell on her, but they kept their distance and didn't ask questions. For that, she was grateful. Others seemed to respect his privacy because of his attitude.

At that thought, she stumbled. No, she was *not* grateful for his attitude because she damn well knew *why* he had it. Bile filled her throat, and she swallowed it back.

She loved him.

That was the only reason she could think of that she'd be feeling this way. Because if she were honest with herself, she'd gladly give up her happiness with him—something she was already doing—if she could make it so he didn't have to live with the pain that scarred him. Her hands shook as the revelation hit her.

If Mitchell had still been mated to Heather, if somehow the other woman had become a wolf and her mating bond to Mitchell held true, then he wouldn't have lived through the pain that forever shadowed his soul.

And Dawn wouldn't know he was her potential.

A mate that would never be hers.

There would be no bond.

There would be no future.

And, somehow, Dawn had to remind herself that she'd gone into everything in the past few weeks knowing that was the case.

"Dawn?"

She froze at the sound of Mitchell's voice and looked up. Somehow, she'd kept walking toward Brie's home but hadn't made it there. Instead, she stood near a group of trees along the path, her palms sweaty and her heart aching.

"Dawn?" he asked again, this time coming right up to her and running his hands down her arms. This was why she kept falling deeper and deeper for him. Because no matter how much he tried to keep his distance, he was always there to make sure she was safe. He constantly touched her, a little caress here, a gentle graze there. It was as if his wolf and his human half didn't understand that they needed to keep each other in check. But Dawn was doing exactly the same damn thing, so she couldn't blame them. She couldn't even blame herself.

She could only blame fate.

Again.

"Sorry," she said, shaking her head. "Woolgathering." *Falling in love with the wrong man.*

He tucked a piece of her hair behind her ear and frowned. "You look sad. Is something wrong in your den?"

She started to shake her head, then stopped. "Not really. Everything's just so new." She looked over her shoulder, aware they'd caught the attention of a few wolves going about their business. "I shouldn't speak about it here, though."

Mitchell looked her over before giving her a tight nod. "Let's head back to my place and talk."

She shook her head fully this time. "I can't. I told Brie I'd stop by her place."

"She can wait if you need time to center yourself."

Dawn blew out a breath and took a step back from him. It was hard to ground herself with him touching her. "I don't want to be rude, and I think seeing Fallon might help."

He met her gaze before giving her a nod. "When you're done, though, come to my place."

She raised a brow at the order in his voice. "You're not my Beta, Mitchell. Watch the tone."

His lips quirked into a smile. "I thought you liked the tone."

When she rolled her eyes, he leaned forward and captured her lips—in full view of his Pack. Her heart sped up before squeezing far too tightly.

She'd have to back away soon. Leave him and what they were doing to each other behind if she wanted to keep any part of herself whole in the end.

But for tonight, she'd have him, if only for a few breaths.

"I need to go, but I'll stop by your house on my way out. You'll be there?"

He studied her face before nodding. "I have some paperwork to go over, so I'll be in my home office. You can walk in whenever you're ready." He paused. "I keyed you in so you don't have to knock."

He was killing her one generous moment at a time.

"Thanks," she said softly, her throat tight. "I, uh...will see you soon." She didn't run from him, but it was close. Perhaps if others hadn't been around, she'd have moved even faster, but there was only so much embarrassment and pity she could take. And it *was* pity, she knew. Oh, sure, the others around them didn't know that Mitchell had already been mated and lost his other half, but they knew something was *off*, knew there was no mating bond between Mitchell and her, even though it was obvious there was more than simple attraction.

Yet she'd only done this to herself and, therefore, only had herself to blame.

Brie stood on the porch when Dawn came into view of the Alpha's home. The other woman gave her a soft look before walking down the path toward her. Without saying a word, she held out Fallon, who smiled widely at Dawn and reached out with her chubby, little arms. As soon as Fallon's soft weight hit Dawn's chest, her wolf immediately perked up, pressing slightly into her skin.

"You looked like you needed that," Brie said with a small smile. "Come on in. I have cupcakes and tea."

"Cupcakes?" Dawn asked, kissing Fallon's plump cheek.

"Frosting makes everything better." They walked inside together, Fallon in her arms and Brie by her side. They sat down on the couch, ate too much frosting, and drank some tea while Fallon ate a soft cookie.

After the adults had talked for a while about trivial things that calmed Dawn enough so she could breathe again, the little girl put her hands on Dawn's cheeks and pressed her forehead to hers. Immediately, Dawn's wolf perked up even more and sat in awe of the quiet power of this young pup.

This was what Dawn had been missing, not the daughter of the Alpha, a future leader in her own right, but the presence of a soft soul that needed comfort and guidance. It would be years, if not more, before the Centrals were ready for that step, meaning Dawn would stay in this state of limbo until that happened.

Her wolf held back a whimper, and Dawn sighed, hugging Fallon close.

She was a ball of emotions lately, and she wasn't sure she liked it. No, she was pretty sure she hated it.

"I need to put Fallon down for her nap," Brie said a few minutes later. "Will you be here when I get back, or are you headed to Mitchell's?"

Dawn picked at her jeans, trying to figure out her answer. "I think I need to go to Mitchell's."

Brie stepped forward as Dawn stood, Fallon in her arms with her head resting on her mother's shoulder. "I wish there was something I could do for you both. I *know* you're hurting, just like he is, and I know he's been hurting for a while. Maybe since I met him. I also know it's not my place to ask *why*." She licked her lips and met Dawn's gaze. "He told us," she whispered. "About Heather. He didn't mention your name, but I know, honey."

Dawn's heart sped up, and tears pricked at her eyes. "He told me he was going to tell Max. I didn't know he told everyone else."

"Just the family."

But the Brentwoods were a large family, so that meant Mitchell was finally able to reveal his secret and release some of his burdens.

"Did everyone react okay?" She bit her lip, annoyed with herself for even daring to say that aloud. She wasn't Pack, nor was she family, and, technically, she had no right to stand up for Mitchell. But she didn't want to see him hurt any more—especially by family members who might not even know they were doing it.

"They didn't attack him, if that's what you mean," Brie said softly. She rocked back and forth, a sleepy Fallon yawning in her arms. "I think we all knew there was *something* in his past holding him back from fully being in the here and now. Though I don't know what haunts him more, losing Heather, or knowing he would have lost her anyway because of age." Brie's eyes filled, and Dawn shook her head.

"I...I need to go." She couldn't stand there and see the pity in Brie's eyes. The other woman didn't mean anything by it, but it still hurt.

"Of course. But, Dawn? I'm here for you. No matter what."

Dawn nodded and walked out, but knew that the last part wasn't quite true. Mitchell was Pack, *family*. Dawn was just a new friend that kept showing up in their den. Once again, Dawn felt lost and hated that she kept putting herself in this position. If she were smart, she'd get in her vehicle, head out of the den, and never come back.

Only she knew she wouldn't be smart.

Not tonight.

CHAPTER SIXTEEN

Though Mitchell had left the door open for her, Dawn still knocked, apparently not ready to take that step. He had a feeling she may not ever be ready if they remained in this broken fragment of a relationship.

When he answered the door, a frown on his face, he immediately pulled her into his arms. She wrapped herself around him, inhaling his scent and pressing her cheek to the soft cotton of his well-worn shirt.

"You told them," she whispered. "Are you okay?"

He closed the door behind her and kissed the top of her head, all the while keeping his hold on her. "I should have told them long ago." He tightened his arms around her. "They don't hate me." He swallowed hard. "I thought they would hate me."

"For keeping your secret? No. They might be disappointed, but they can't hate you for what you had to do. Everyone keeps secrets when there isn't another option."

"I lost her," he said after a moment, his words heavy. "It's been so long that I can barely see her face without thinking really hard."

Dawn stilled in his arms, and he felt like a fool for talking about his dead mate with Dawn in his arms. Goddess, he was going to Hell for sure.

"Shit, I'm sorry."

"No, you need to talk about her." She cleared her throat and took a few steps away. His wolf mourned the loss, and Mitchell knew if he weren't careful, he'd hurt Dawn more than he ever thought possible.

"I did my talking." He cupped her face. "Why don't you talk to me about what's going on with you? Are you still feeling left out within the Pack?"

She sighed. "Yeah, and I hate myself a little more each day because of it. So what if the moon goddess didn't give me a title? It doesn't make me any less the wolf I was before."

He nodded, understanding. "Your Pack is still finding its place. There will always be that part of its memory trying to atone for what happened before you were even born. Add in the fact that you're a maternal without children in the den, and there's reason for you to feel a bit off. You shouldn't feel bad."

She gave him a self-deprecating smile. "You know, it never used to be an issue before I came to your den. I think it was easier before I knew what I was missing."

"It'll come," he said softly, unsure how to help her.

"I know. And I know I just need to remain strong and do what I've always done. I guess I just needed a little pity party." She gave him a wide smile that didn't quite reach her eyes. "I guess that's why I'm happy you're my friend. It gives me someone to talk to who isn't Pack."

It was a shot to the heart, and they both knew it. But if they didn't keep their boundaries clear, it would hurt more later.

Of course, that was all a lie, and he needed to back the fuck away. So, of course, that's why he leaned forward and kissed her, hard. "Come to bed with me," he said softly. "I'll make sure you're taken care of."

"Oh, yeah?" she asked, her wolf in her eyes. "So, sex is how I can get over the whole new Pack thing?"

He nibbled down her neck. He couldn't figure out who had attacked her in that alley, didn't know who had come after his Pack, he also didn't know what he was going to do about his own choices since his wolf *still* wouldn't think about a true mating. What he *could* do was distract her.

"It might help. Let's try it out and see."

She laughed, and he knew the human part of him had fallen in love with her.

If only his wolf would get on board.

"And maybe we should try more than once. Just for practice." Her eyes danced this time, and he picked her up, carrying her to the bedroom as she laughed. They were complicating their ties even more, but he couldn't back away. Maybe if he kept holding her, kept loving her, his wolf would understand why they were ready to take the next step.

Maybe.

Somehow, even though they tried to keep their hands on each other the entire time, they stripped out of their clothes and lay naked face-to-face on his bed, slowly trailing their hands over one another. Each time they'd been together before, it was fast, almost too quick for him to learn every curve of her, ever dip and valley.

The human part of him never wanted to let her go, wanted to finish what they'd started and take a step he might regret *not* taking.

His wolf half thought of it as a betrayal—though...not as much as it had before.

It was no wonder he was constantly conflicted when it came to the woman in his arms, in his bed.

He brushed his fingers along the swell of her breast, luxuriating in the way her nipple pebbled by just the barest graze of his touch. He bent forward and took that peak into his mouth, knowing the stubble of his beard scraped along her soft skin. However, he *also* knew she loved when he did that, so he purposely hadn't shaved. She'd slowly become part of his daily routine, had affected small aspects of his life without even trying. Though he wasn't sure what he would do about the larger picture, for now, he planned to take in the smaller moments and know that it was just now part of who he was.

Their hands slid over one another as he rolled so he hovered above her and moved between her legs.

"I need you," she whispered, her eyes wide and dark. "I...I need you. Please."

He lowered his head and kissed her. "You never have to beg." He swallowed hard, emotion a hard knot in his throat. "Do I need to find a condom?"

It was a step. Progress in a direction where they would only have one more chance after tonight to back out. The human part of him *needed* to form a bond with this woman, needed that connection. His wolf half might be holding back, but he knew this was the time his human half had been waiting for.

In all the years he'd been alone and in mourning, he'd been waiting for Dawn. She was his light, his next step.

He just hoped they weren't making a mistake.

"I want you now." She licked her lips. "Just you."

He let out a shuddering breath, then slowly, oh so slowly, slid inside her. Without a barrier, he knew he'd found his slice of Heaven.

"Goddess," Dawn whispered below him. "I...I never knew."

He kissed her, needing her lips, her taste. "I need to move. Are you ready for me?"

Her eyes opened then, meeting his gaze. "Always."

Then he *moved.*

Though they'd started slow, there was nothing leisurely about how they moved now. She arched her hips for him, meeting him thrust for thrust as he slammed into her over and over again, his cock going so deep he knew they'd both be sore in the morning. He pulled back and tucked up one of her knees so it pressed close to her chest and gave him an even *deeper* angle. And when she reached around him and grabbed his ass, squeezing him tightly, he knew he wouldn't last much longer.

So he rolled over again, letting her ride him so he could watch her breasts sway and her mouth part.

And when he came, the first part of the mating bond snapped into place, however frail and incomplete it might be.

"Mitchell—" she whispered.

"Mine—" he said at the same time.

Their bodies shook, and he knew that they might have just made a horrible mistake. Because even though both Dawn and he had told themselves they didn't need a mate, they'd been lying. He'd lost one mate, and now, if he wasn't careful, he could lose another. Their human halves had bonded. Now, it was up to their wolves and everything else going on around them to see if it stuck.

They were mates, yet not.

Connected, yet set apart.

Broken, yet with the possibility of being whole.

He held Dawn close and inhaled her sweetly crisp scent. He had no idea what they were going to do next, but he had a feeling, no matter what, what they'd done tonight would have consequences that could last beyond the fading wisp of a bond's beginning.

The next day, Mitchell rubbed the back of his neck, a sense of dread coating his stomach. He didn't get whispered words from the moon goddess, and he sure as hell wasn't a foreseer, but he had a bad feeling about today.

"What's up with you?" Max asked from his side. The two of them were on patrol duty that afternoon since the soldier that usually worked with Max was at home with his pup that broke her leg while trying to climb trees. They were wolves, not cats, and some young ones—hell, some not so young ones—tended to forget that.

At that thought, he frowned. Were there cat pups? No, they'd probably be called cubs, right? And the Aspens were called a Pack since they were known to their world as wolves, but were there all-cat *Prides* out there somewhere? He'd only begun to think about the ramifications of what Audrey told them, and he knew if he weren't so distracted with Dawn, he might have made more sense of everything.

"Okay, now your face looks like you're trying to do math. Never try to do math, Mitch. You know how much it hurts you."

For a moment, Max sounded like his old self, and Mitchell almost tripped as he looked over at his brother. Max's face didn't show any of the light that had sounded with that statement, but Mitchell had *heard* it. It had to count for something.

"I was just thinking about cats and Prides and naming." He shrugged but kept his voice down. They were alone for now, but he didn't want his voice to carry. Until they knew to do with the information, Gideon had chosen not to inform the rest of the Pack—including the elders—about the existence of other shifters. Doing so might threaten Audrey's life, and do more harm than good, so Mitchell agreed with the decision.

Max snorted, even as he kept his eyes on the perimeter. They weren't at war at the moment, but with the rogue attacks and things still so new with the human factions, their wolves were still cautious.

"You know," his brother began, "I'm still not sure what to do with that information. I don't know why Audrey wanted us in the loop on that particular secret."

Mitchell had been thinking about that, as well—when he wasn't tossing and turning, dealing with the fact that his wolf and his human half didn't seem to agree on much these days.

"I'm not sure either, but if the moon goddess whispered it into her ear, then it must have been for a reason."

Max shook his head. "The moon goddess seems to be talking to us a lot more these days. Well, not *us* since I'm pretty sure you and I are the only two wolves—or cats—left in existence who don't seem to be on a first-name basis with her."

Mitchell couldn't help but smile at that. "It sure seems like it, doesn't it?"

The two of them patrolled in silence for a while after that, no words needing to be spoken, as they were both lost to their thoughts and troubles. He wished he could help his brother, but there was nothing he could do except be there when Max needed him. As for Mitchell, well, he had his own problems to sort out. The night before had changed everything with Dawn, and they both knew it.

Their human halves had made the decision for them, but their wolf halves hadn't yet accepted their fate. More accurately, *his* wolf hadn't marked Dawn as his. What frustrated him to no end was that it was their wolves to begin with that had sent them through the mating dance. Without their shifter halves, they would probably be attracted to each other, but there wouldn't be this burning need for *more*. Yet when the time came to take that step and get over the past, his wolf held him back.

And a part of Mitchell knew that Dawn's wolf did the same. Only, he had a feeling it was because her wolf was protecting Dawn's human heart. He'd always known it would be complicated considering who they were, but he never knew it would be like *this*.

"I know I'm the last person who should be saying this..." Max cursed under his breath and then started again. "But, Mitch? You need to do what feels right *now*, rather than fear for the future or let the past take over. I wish you'd have told me about Heather when it first happened, but I get why you didn't. Yet despite all that, it's been *decades* since you lost her. Would she have wanted you to wear your hair shirt as you are, pushing away the one woman who could help you live your life to the fullest? Dawn is a wolf, just like you. You won't lose her to old age. Yes, in our long lives, we're more likely to be injured or killed by another wolf's hand because of the way we live and function within a Pack, but she'd have that as a Central or your mate. Danger is part of our lives, but hope? That doesn't come often. Don't lose her because you're afraid."

Mitchell swallowed hard, knowing Max wasn't only talking about Dawn, yet there wasn't anything else he could say, not when they both had their own demons to face.

The thing was, Mitchell had already chosen to have Dawn in his life. He'd seen the person she was and had glimpsed the woman she could become. He *loved* the fierce protectiveness that coated her every movement and decision. He wanted that as part of his life, and some part of him told him that Dawn hadn't been goddess-blessed as a Central because she was meant to be a Talon.

They'd slept together the night before without a condom, his seed spilling deep inside her, cementing the human half of their bond, but it wasn't enough. Already, he could feel the fading warmth of the woman that could be his because there was no mating mark tying them together. Without his wolf's bite— without *her* wolf's bite—the fragile connection they shared would fade to dust, and they would be forced to walk away from each other. He wasn't sure he could do that, yet he didn't know if his wolf could get over losing Heather.

Fate wasn't a blessing, it was a curse.

Before Mitchell could lament for too much longer about his own failings, Kameron and Walker came over the tree line and headed their way. Max shrank into himself like he did whenever he was around more than one person these days, and Mitchell had a feeling it was also because Walker had spent so much of his time lately trying to heal the worst of Max's scars. Normally, his brother should have lost at least some of them by now, but for some reason, they weren't healing, and it just was more evidence, at least to Max, that he needed to stay hidden.

Mitchell held back a growl at that and wanted to kick something. Between Dawn and Max, he was about to go out of his mind not being able to do what he needed to protect those he cared about.

"Hey, we passed by Gwen on our way over, and she mentioned that Dawn was stopping by to help at the daycare center once she finished work at the café," Walker said in lieu of a greeting.

Mitchell nodded and checked his phone. "She should be over soon then." He lifted his chin at his cousins even as they started their way to the front gate to finish up their patrol. Walker and Kameron would most likely be taking over unless Kameron had someone else on shift. "Dawn said she was going to quit her volunteer work at the human daycare center since they didn't really need her and that she was pretty sure they were just placating her." He let out a small growl. "She was also worried about what the parents might think since, apparently, word of her being a shifter got out."

"Fuck," Kameron growled low. "I thought we caught all the security cameras and witnesses."

"You might have," Mitchell agreed, "but someone talked."

"How's her job at the café then?" Walker asked. "Her boss and coworkers upset?"

"Not that I know of," Mitchell answered as he leapt over a fallen log. "I'm keeping an eye on it, though."

Max gave him a knowing look, and Mitchell bared his fangs. The other two didn't comment on it, but he knew they were paying attention. Not only were they too worried about Max, but they also probably had a million questions and concerns about Mitchell and Dawn.

And as soon as Mitchell had answers, he'd probably still keep them guessing until he was alone with Dawn.

As if conjuring her, he caught sight of her vehicle driving down the road on the outside of the den. His wolf brushed along his skin, wanting to get closer. Yet, because his wolf was an asshole, it didn't want to get *too* close and betray the ghost of a bond it had with Heather.

Fucking wolf.

He was about to raise his hand in a wave but froze as the hairs on the back of his neck stood on end. His wolf seemed to know there was something wrong before he did.

The explosion rocked the four men, and Mitchell slammed into the ground with Max, Kameron, and Walker landing around him. The others scrambled to their feet as Mitchell's hands shook and he tried to blink the soot out of his face, keeping his eyes on Dawn's car. She'd come to a stop as soon as whatever exploded had sent the men flying, but Mitchell knew it wasn't the end of it.

He forced himself to a standing position, shouting for her to get down, but it was too late.

He was always too late.

Fire circled them, fire that wasn't natural or man-made, not with the way it licked and danced along his skin and made a perfect perimeter around them. He tried to jump through the flames, even as Dawn ran toward them. Walker shouted, but he couldn't hear what his cousin said, his attention on the woman who had taken part of his heart. Now, he might lose her—just as he'd lost another.

It was all too familiar.

The car.

He looked down at his hands for a brief instant, the blood.

The screams.

The pain.

Fire engulfed Dawn's car in the next moment, and Mitchell tore through the flames, the scent of burning flesh filling his nostrils. The others were right behind him, not caring that they got burned right along with him.

He needed to get to Dawn, needed to see if she'd made it out alive. Only when the flames died down as quickly as they'd come, the car was still on fire...and Dawn was nowhere to be seen.

She was gone.

Others shouted around them, and Mitchell felt Walker press his hands over Mitchell's back, the warmth of his Healing touch soothing rather than scorching like whatever witch or demon had made that flame a moment ago.

"Follow the bond," Max ground out. He turned to see his brother, soot-covered and badly burned on his arm. Walker would fix that. He had to.

"There's no bond," Mitchell rasped. "We're not mated."

"But you have *something*," Kameron growled before shouting at his men to scout the perimeter. "We all scented it when we saw you today. Look deep inside, fucking control that wolf of yours, and save your damned mate!"

It was the most emotion Mitchell had ever seen or heard coming from Kameron, and that spurred Mitchell on, urging him to close his eyes and focus on the wisp of a bond that had been fading every hour since he kissed Dawn goodbye after they made love.

There.

"I have it," he coughed, his lungs slightly singed. "It's weak, but I have it."

"Then let's go get your girl," Max said as Walker Healed Max's arm. "Whoever has been attacking us little by little has one powerful witch on their side."

"Should we bring Leah?" Walker asked, sweat covering his face. His cousin could Heal others, but not himself. For that, they would need Leah, a healing water witch, but that wasn't what Mitchell thought Walker was talking about.

"She's not strong enough since the birth. She needs time to gather her strength. And I'm not going to put her in danger when we don't know what we're up against." He paused, his wolf restless. "You should stay behind, too. Heal."

Walker shook his head. "You might need me." They didn't mention that since Dawn wasn't a Talon, Walker couldn't help her if things were too far gone, but there was one way she could become a Talon. And that was something Mitchell was prepared for, even if it had taken far too long for his wolf to get on board. "I'm not burned. It's just my lungs. I'll be fine. Kameron took the brunt of it." He glared at his triplet, and the Enforcer shrugged.

"You can Heal me. Not yourself. My men are on guard duty and letting Gideon and Cole know what's up. While they're doing that, the four of us are heading out. Ready?"

Mitchell's wolf growled, and he nodded, beyond ready to fight for his *mate*.

Someone had dared to take Dawn from him, and for that, they would pay.

No matter how much hell he had to rain down for that to happen.

CHAPTER SEVENTEEN

D awn's head ached as she tried to open her
eyes. Her lids felt heavy, and her body even
heavier, but she finally managed to pry open
her eyelids, only to close them again when the
bright light above proved overwhelming.

She moaned, her wolf trying to get out to help her,
only somehow too lethargic to help at all. The smell of
cabin smoke and an acrid taste coated her tongue, and
she couldn't understand what that scent could be.

"Oh, good, you're awake."

The smoky voice sounded almost bored from the
way she spoke, and Dawn finally opened her eyes fully
to see a tall woman with ruby red hair and lips to
match. She leaned over Dawn and blinked slowly. It
was only then that Dawn realized she was strapped to
a wooden bench inside an old—and clearly abandoned
from the layers of dust and cobwebs—log cabin.

Her eyes went to the corner where Sam hovered,
his ankles and wrists in manacles. Dawn let out a
whimper at the sight of her friend so still, so pale. She
hadn't seen him since the day before, and now...and

now she couldn't breathe, couldn't quite focus or understand what she was seeing.

The chains that held Sam down were no longer connected to the wall.

Nothing held him back.

Nothing except death.

That was what she'd scented.

The acrid taste of death.

"Where am I?" Dawn asked, her voice hoarse. She didn't know if it was from screaming when she'd seen Mitchell and his family go down in flames, or from the smoke itself. Either way, she knew this woman and her unkind eyes could be the last things she saw if she weren't careful. And she couldn't let her know how much pain she was in at seeing Sam. Her body ached and her heart shuddered.

Sam.

Sam was gone.

Forever.

And there was nothing she could do.

She couldn't grieve. She couldn't comprehend.

The witch, or perhaps the wolves around the cabin, had killed Sam before Dawn had even been taken to the house from the scent of things, and yet Dawn didn't understand what was going on.

"Where no one will find you," the witch answered. Because this woman had to be a witch, her magic tasted of it. And since the fire that had come out of nowhere seemed so unnatural, Dawn was betting she was a fire witch.

The woman laughed suddenly, and Dawn forced herself not to react.

"That sounded ominous, didn't it?" She shrugged a slender shoulder, looking oddly graceful as she did it. "Anyway, I'm not exactly sure where we are. I only know that I'm supposed to keep you here for a bit."

She sighed and leaned back so Dawn had a better view of her surroundings. She couldn't really tell anything other than it was a place she'd never scented before and there was no way, at least at the moment, she'd be able to undo the thick leather straps keeping her bound to the table.

Her heart sped up, and she tried to focus on what she was going to do next. She couldn't move, nor did she think screaming for help would help her in any way. Her bonds with her Pack were so new that she wasn't sure they would work if she tugged on them. But she'd try.

The same could be said for the soft, fading bond that she had with Mitchell.

She still *felt* the bond that wasn't supposed to be there with him. That meant he was alive...right? She swallowed through the thick knot in her throat and hoped that the witch couldn't sense feelings or thoughts like some witches could. Hopefully, she only thought Dawn was scared, not worried about the man she loved. Because she had a feeling if this woman thought she could use Mitchell against Dawn, then she would. That was if she wasn't already using Dawn against Mitchell.

"What do you want?" Dawn asked.

"Me? Nothing. I'm just waiting." The woman snapped her fingers, and a small ball of flame danced along her knuckles. For a moment, Dawn thought she scented a familiar Pack beneath the ash and flame, but she couldn't focus on that. Not then. Maybe not ever. "And I hate to be kept waiting."

Dawn's scream echoed through the room as the first flame kissed her skin. This time, she knew why her throat hurt and figured she'd lose her voice entirely. She just prayed the tugs and pulls she sent along the few bonds she had would be enough.

The witch tilted her head at her and blinked, the flame ending quickly. "You scream, and yet...I feel hope radiating from you. It's as if you're sure you'll be saved."

This woman was clearly a sociopath. It was as if she felt nothing but mimicked those around her in order to feel something other than the flame that danced along her eyes and skin.

She smiled suddenly but it didn't reach her eyes and that worried Dawn beyond the flame. "Henry. Jacob."

The two men who had been prowling outside of the cabin walked into to the room, their eyes glowing gold from their wolves, their naked chests heaving. Dawn didn't recognize them but knew they were wolves who were on the brink of their control or perhaps far beyond that line. They didn't scent of Pack and she didn't know what that meant other than whoever held their leashes wasn't doing a good enough job at keeping them sane.

"Now boys, no blood and no cuts. We don't want her to end everything too quickly, but perhaps a nibble or two will help make sure this young one understands there can be no hope for her not anymore. And, young one? If you shift, I will kill you and make it hurt more than I'd planned. I might even let the boys have a bite or two just to prove to you that you made a mistake about siding with the wrong wolf."

Dawn struggled against her bonds and the witch shook her head, her long red hair flowing down her back. This woman scared her, as did the two wolves prowling toward her, but none of them were what truly scared her.

Someone else was behind all of this. Someone else held the reins. And though the witch might be right and there might not be hope for herself, there was still hope for the Centrals, the Talons...the Redwoods.

And Dawn *knew* that whoever had orchestrated all of this had far more plans than hurting a single wolf of a newly formed Pack.

Far more.

And this time, when she screamed, it wasn't only for her, but for what was to come.

For her friends.

For her Pack.

For Mitchell.

The second time Dawn woke, she could barely keep her eyes open. Her body ached, and she knew without a Healer, she'd succumb and give in to whatever this witch wanted. Only her Pack didn't have a Healer, and witches who could help were few and far between.

The witch that was in the cabin with her was not one of those witches.

Or rather, had been in the room with her.

Dawn closed her eyes, taking a deep breath to get through the worst of the pain, and then tried to look around the small dwelling that had been her cage for the past couple of hours. She could scent the other woman, but it was fading, telling her that whoever the redhead was, she was no longer in the room.

Instead, at least two male wolves in human form prowled outside the cabin, leaving Dawn alone and still strapped to the wooden bench. Exhausted and fearing that no one was close enough to feel anything she'd done with the bonds, she tried to calm herself.

Her wolf had come to the surface during the witch's games, taking the brunt of the attack for her, and because of that, it now lay far beneath Dawn's skin, tucked tight in a ball and trying to heal itself.

Only Dawn didn't know if she had enough energy for that.

Tears pricked at her eyes, but she blinked them back. She would *not* go down without a fight. Using the last of her strength, she pulled at her bound arms, trying to lift them. When the leather began to give, she let the tears fall.

The witch had used fire on Dawn's skin, and in so doing, she had weakened the strength of the leather.

Dawn never thought she'd be grateful for inept torturing.

And from that thought, she knew her mind was clearly on the edge of a break. All she wanted was to go back home and hug her parents. She wanted to make her mom coffee and kiss the top of her dad's head. She wanted her brother to growl at her for something silly, and then she wanted to go off to work so she could see Cheyenne, Aimee, and Dhani while eating biscotti with bacon on the side.

She wanted to run into Mitchell's arms and have him hold her and tell her everything would be okay.

She wanted the bond to be real.

But since she was alone in the cabin, alone for far more than she bargained for, she knew she had to be tough. She was a maternal dominant, and that meant she could heal faster than many wolves. She would use that to her advantage.

She just needed to get off this bench.

With immense effort, she tugged and pulled at the restraints until she was able to move her hands just enough that she could let her claws slide through her fingertips. As soon as she did that, her breath caught, adrenaline coursing through her system.

Going slowly as not to make a silly mistake or too much noise and alert the two wolves on guard, she somehow tore through the rest of the restraints and forced herself to a seated position. Her skin stung, the wounds far deeper than she'd thought at first, but she ignored all of that. If she could somehow get out of this, she'd find someone to help her. She didn't care what she looked like, she just needed to be alive.

Dawn was just about to slide off the bench when the door opened. Instead of freezing like she almost did, she rolled off to the side, her body screaming at her for daring such a move. The two men scrambled into the room, claws out and fangs bared.

She did the same, but knew she was no match for these two. Healthy, she might have been able to take them since she was more dominant, but she was far from okay right then.

When they jumped toward her, growling, she shifted to the side, tears streaming down her face as she tried to ignore the fiery pain radiating through her body. She slashed one of the guys down the side with her claws, but the other, who had fully shifted, bit her leg.

She screamed, trying to fight them both off, but knew it was useless.

Once more, she pushed at the bonds within her, begging someone for help. She would go down fighting, but unless someone came for her, she would *go down.*

As soon as she touched the bond with Mitchell, *she knew.*

He stormed through the door, breaking it off its hinges as he landed on the ground. Max was by his side and jumped on the back of one of the wolves coming at her. Dawn crawled out of the way, but kept her claws out, ready to fight, but as soon as the Brentwoods entered the small cabin, it was over.

The two wolves who scented of no Pack and hadn't spoken a single word to her were no match for the Talons. There were sounds of fighting outside that told her she'd missed a few guards when she tried to scent them and couldn't help but be grateful for whoever had come to help Mitchell.

She leaned with her back against the wall and tried to take in deep breaths, only she couldn't. She was fading fast, but couldn't help but be grateful for all the training she'd had. She hadn't backed down, hadn't stopped trying to save herself.

Only it seemed she was too late.

Knowing she needed to conserve her energy, she closed her eyes, only to be startled awake as Mitchell held her in his arms on his lap.

"Dawn? Baby? Don't close your eyes. I need you to look at me." Tears filled his eyes, and his wolf was at the surface since he had a gold rim around his irises. "Walker's right here, but he can't Heal you. We can patch you up medically, but..." His voice cracked.

"It won't be enough," Walker continued, speaking for the man she loved. "I can only Heal you if you're a Talon."

And she could only be a Talon if the Alpha brought her in...and since he wasn't near, and she didn't know how that would work anyway since she'd basically just become a Central and Pack bonds were tricky, there was only one other thing she could do.

Accept a mating bond with Mitchell.

Something he hadn't wanted before this and now would be forced into.

Goddess...

How had it come to this? How had all of their agonizing and denials come down to a decision that no one should be forced to make?

"Baby? I can't take this choice from you..."

At Mitchell's words, it hit her how similar this situation must be for him. He'd been forced to let one mate die because he couldn't force her shift, not that he'd known whether it would work in the first place.

She tried to open her mouth to tell him that she loved him, that she wanted to be his mate, only she couldn't speak.

Mitchell let out an agonized snarl and took a deep breath. "Baby, please."

In answer, she tilted her head to the side and, using the last of her energy, put her hand over his heart, her palm bloody and scorched. Her fingers dug into his chest as she tried to pull him toward her, but she didn't have the strength.

"Damn it," he growled. "I love you too much to let you go. Forgive me," he whispered. "Forgive me." Then he brought her closer and bit into her shoulder, his fangs sliding into the flesh of her neck.

Her wolf raised her head and howled...the bond that brought two souls together cementing in a cascade of sparks and light. Kameron and Max surrounded them, their wolves in their eyes as they howled for her, as well. This was supposed to be a private moment, an intimate matter, but right then, all Dawn could think of was Mitchell.

There was nothing to forgive, and she prayed he understood.

She could *feel* him within her, their souls blending as one before settling into their own skins. At the same time, the bond between her and the Centrals broke, a slingshot of pain before she landed safely within the Talon's embrace. She could sense Gideon holding onto her for dear life, his massive paw wrapped around the bond that now connected her to his Pack as he kept her steady enough for Walker.

And through it all, Mitchell held her close, lapping up the wound on her neck as he made her his.

They'd already connected their human halves, and now their wolves had done the same.

Walker used his powers to Heal her, though she couldn't feel him, she could only focus on Mitchell.

Her mate.

Her love.

Her future.

The man who loved her as much as she loved him.

The one man who she thought would always be too far away, too broken for her to bare witness.

And now, he was hers.

Warmly wrapped in her lover's embrace, she let the Talons bring her into the fold, knowing this was only the beginning. They still needed to find out who had hurt her, and she had more questions than answers, but for now, she knew she would have the *time* to ask them.

For now, she wasn't just Dawn, a woman in need of saving. She had fought to save herself and had then given in when others offered to help. That was far more than she'd ever done before. She could see now that she would have a purpose, a new life with her new Pack and the man she loved.

And she'd do everything in her power to ensure that no one in this room or out of it regretted the decisions made.

She was no longer the daughter of the daughter of the daughter of disgrace.

She was Dawn. Former Central. New Talon.

And mated.

A title she could live with...as long as she could *live*.

CHAPTER EIGHTEEN

D awn took a deep breath and looked down at her hands, stretching her fingers and joints, trying to remember exactly how she'd come to be here. She wore Mitchell's shirt that went halfway down her thighs and covered the worst of her healing burns and cuts. The witch had left her pants alone mostly except for a few tears on her calves, so other than the dirt on her face and the shell-shocked expression, she didn't look too bad.

Mitchell turned off the engine once they pulled up near the Central wards before lifting her up into his arms and settling her onto his lap. He was oh so careful not to hurt her, and she couldn't help but relish the warmth that spread through her at his touch.

He was her *mate.*

She'd known for so long that they had the potential, but she'd never known what it truly meant until she opened herself up to him and he wrapped his soul around hers, a comforting blanket of warmth and protection.

And while that was true, she knew her soul was doing the same to him. He would always be more dominant than her in terms of their wolves, but they were equal in every other way. They complemented each other like they would with no other person in the world.

They were *mates*.

And at that thought, her heart sped up even as she wiped away a tear. Her heart was so full, yet it hurt for what she'd lost...what she'd almost lost.

"Are you hurting? We can go right back to the den and see Walker. You should be resting, my mate." His lips brushed along her skin, and she sank into him.

"My body's fine, and my soul touches yours, but my heart?" She wiped away a tear. "Sam." The tears fell freely at her pack mate's name. "I can't believe he's gone. He was my friend, and he's gone because of me."

He'd never find his mate, never come to know his wolf and the strength he'd hidden for so long. No one would ever know if he would have become a full Omega or learn some new power that would show the world whom he truly was.

Sam never had an unkind word for anyone, and yet they'd stolen his life from him.

His future.

His hope.

Had he screamed for her? Had he felt any pain?

He'd been alone...and she hadn't been fast enough to save him. She'd been so in her head with her own worries that she hadn't known he was missing.

No one had.

Mitchell's chest rumbled with a deep growl, and her wolf pressed into her skin, needing to be closer. "It wasn't your fault. It was that witch and those she worked with." He growled low, his fangs brushing along her skin along with his breath. "We'll find them and figure out why they did what they did. I'll rip the witch limb from limb for daring to touch you. For daring to take Sam." He growled. "For daring to cross the boundaries."

"How...I know Sam wasn't the same as Heather in terms of what he was to me, but how can you get through so much loss? You've lost so much, and I don't know how you do it." If she hadn't been able to feel his soul through hers, she'd never have asked the question, but she knew there would be no secrets between them.

"You breathe through it and know that it will take time." He shook his head. "I spent so long pushing away so much of what I could feel because I was afraid to let that hurt happen again. Whatever you need to do in order to grieve your friend, know I'm here for you."

They were quiet for a moment before she nuzzled into him. "I know you said Kameron and Walker called my brother to tell him you found me and Sam," she shuddered, swallowing hard, "but did you say anything else?"

"Walker is taking care of Sam's body," he whispered, and she sucked in a sob. "He'll make sure Sam is ready to be seen by his family since you don't have a Healer yet. I didn't talk to your brother personally, but he had to have felt you leave the Centrals and come to the Talons when we bonded." He paused and ran a hand through her hair. "He'd have felt when he lost a Pack member, though not to the degree he'd have felt losing Sam. We'll make sure that he knows we're all here for him if he needs to figure out how to deal with knowing that bond and honoring that memory."

Before she could say anything, though, she caught her family's scent on the wind, and she sat up, wincing as the movement pulled at her healing wounds. "They know we're here."

Mitchell kissed her temple. "Of course, they do. They've known since we first drove up. Their sentries are getting better with their training."

Another reminder of how she'd met Mitchell and how far her Pack had come in such a short time.

They stepped out of the vehicle, and her parents held out their arms. She ran into their embrace, tears falling freely again, along with theirs, even though they were careful not to squeeze too hard. Though she wasn't part of their Pack anymore and she could no longer feel even the slightest bonds, they would always be her parents. She just hoped they'd understand why she was leaving so soon after their formation.

"Mona. Rand." Mitchell's voice brought her out of her thoughts, and she looked up to see him standing by her brother. "I'm sorry I wasn't fast enough to get her out without harm."

"Mitchell," Dawn put it in. "You just finished telling me that it wasn't my fault, so you can't go on and blame yourself for the same thing."

He narrowed his eyes at her. "It wasn't your fault, but you are my mate. I should protect you."

She gave the healing gash on his arm a pointed look. "You could also say the same for me."

Her father let out a soft chuckle. "I see you two are well matched." Her dad hugged her close before letting her go and walking over to Mitchell with his hand out. "Welcome to the family, son."

Mitchell's eyes widened fractionally, but she wasn't sure anyone else caught it as he gripped her father's hand and shook it. "

"You'll always be a Central, sis," Cole said with a sad smile. "I know you're a Talon now, but we're yours, too. Bond or no bond."

Dawn's heart once again warmed. "I know…I know I haven't always acted like it."

"Honey, that's not true," her mother put in. "You put our people first every day of your life. You worked in a place you didn't love and one that hurt your wolf because you couldn't be with children or help others because you knew our Pack needed to be close and grow. You did all of that because you love us."

Dawn shook her head. "You say that, yet once the bonds came, I never truly fit in, did I? I felt so childish in that I felt as if the moon goddess owed me something." She closed her eyes, a small smile playing on her face despite the seriousness of the conversation around her. "It seemed she knew my purpose had another path other than to be part of the Centrals."

Mitchell held out his arm, and she sank into him. "You're the Beta's mate, and I believe you will one day be lead maternal dominant if Gwen has anything to say about it. You always had a purpose, even if it was a little cloudy for a while."

Cole came forward and brushed his lips along her forehead. "You will *always* be family. Always be my baby sister." He grinned. "And before I force you to sit down inside the house so you can rest and talk some more, there are three other people who have been chomping at the bit to see you."

Dawn froze then turned as Cheyenne, Dhani, and Aimee came running toward her, mixtures of worry, relief, and tenderness on their faces.

Soon, she found herself in the arms of her three best friends, whom she'd forced into this wolf life of hers, and yet she knew there was a reason for that. What, she didn't know, but she had a feeling there would be more to come with her friends and this new world of theirs.

Mitchell stood at her back, her friends surrounding her, and her family with her as well, and she knew she wasn't alone. Even through the pain and loss of the past few hours, she had her hope, her future.

Her path.

Finally.

CHAPTER NINETEEN

Mitchell paced Gideon's living room, his wolf growling at him, when a soft yet strong hand reached out and grasped his wrist.

"Sit down, you're making me dizzy."

As it was his mate who ordered him to do so, he did it without question. He ignored the knowing looks on his family's faces and sat down on the couch next to Dawn before picking her up and gently placing her on his lap.

"I didn't mean that I needed to sit *here*," she said softly, blushing.

He kissed the mating mark he'd placed on her shoulder three days prior and let out a soft growl. "Here is just fine."

Walker chuckled under his breath from the other side of the couch, but Mitchell once again ignored him. He was still riding the mating dance, and the high that came from creating that bond. He still couldn't believe that he and his wolf had taken this long to get their act together.

He would *always* miss Heather and, yes, she'd have a part of his soul until his dying breath, but she was also part of his past—something Dawn understood. It was why she'd stood back for so long while he was a freaking idiot, trying to heal something that wasn't his to heal.

"Mitchell?" his mate whispered. She leaned toward him so only he could hear her in a room full of shifters with superior hearing. "Everything okay?"

He rested his forehead on hers as he forced himself to calm down. Even his wolf paced beneath his skin as it reached out to be near Dawn. He'd almost lost her, not only to the witch and wolves who dared to take her from him, but he almost lost her and this bond because of his fear.

Never again, he reminded himself. Never again would he allow himself to be driven by fear alone.

"I'm good." He kissed her temple, then cleared his throat as his family stared at him. "Okay, I'd be better if we knew who the fuck thinks they can mess with this Pack again."

Kameron issued a growl from the back of his throat. "The wolves that were at that cabin scented of *nothing*."

"That doesn't make any sense," Ryder added. "Lone wolves don't group themselves, they don't form a Pack. Hence the *lone* part."

"These particular ones didn't seem too organized," Walker put in. "Yes, the overall attacks, if pieced together, were organized, but each individual one? Not so much. Someone is controlling these wolves."

Dawn shivered in Mitchell's hold, and he held her closer. "There's also the witch. Whoever is trying to get at the Centrals or the Talons or both has a *very* powerful witch on their side."

Leah, Ryder's mate and a water witch herself, sighed. "And if she's as powerful as I felt when I walked the land she scorched, she's much older than a mere mortal." She met the others' gazes before continuing. "My lifespan increases to match Ryder's, the same as any witch in a shifter Pack."

Mitchell cursed. "Meaning the witch is mated to a wolf to grow in power?"

"That or she was born with the power, but I'm not so sure of that," Leah added.

The others in the room began to add their theories, and Mitchell paid attention but he couldn't help thinking of the way the wolves targeted Dawn so completely.

"Whoever came at us wanted to take out Dawn," Mitchell put in, and the others quieted. "That wolf in the alley kept bypassing me and her human friends to go at her specifically. And she was the one taken by the witch and those wolves."

His arms tightened around her, and he forced himself to loosen his grip.

"Those others came for you, though," Gideon said, his hand over Brie's as he frowned.

Dawn cleared her throat and ducked her head when everyone looked over at her. She wasn't used to being the center of attention, and now that she was a Talon, he knew she had a lot to get used to. He'd help her any way he could, and he already know that Gwen and Brie had decided to take her under their wings.

She'd always have her connection to her family and be an honorary Central member, but now she had more of a Pack to help her wolf. And that meant that no matter what, Mitchell would make sure her former Pack was also taken care of. He never wanted her to regret leaving the Centrals.

"I think that whoever came at us—and I mean *us*—did so because of something greater." She let out a breath, and Mitchell rubbed the small of her back, letting her know he was there. "They took Sam as practice I think. I don't think they had him for long so I think whatever they did to him had to be fast." Her voice cracked, and he wanted to growl for her. "At least...I hope it was fast." She trailed off and he held her closer.

"Go on, baby." His wolf prowled, wanting to know if her thoughts were going in the same direction as his. He had a feeling he knew who was behind it all, and if he were right, this wasn't going to end anytime soon.

"I think they wanted the visible person of the Centrals and Sam might have either gotten in the way or was practice for me, as I said. My brother might be the Alpha, but I was the easiest one to get to. Killing me wouldn't be an outright declaration of war, but it would have hurt my family and the others. As for attacking Mitchell?"

"They wanted to get him out of the way," Kameron growled.

"Make it easier to get to you and, frankly, hurt the Talons for daring to stand in his way."

Max's words filled the room, and Mitchell knew he wasn't the only one who put things together.

"You think it was Blade," Gideon said slowly. Interesting that the Alpha only mentioned the man, not the Pack.

"I do," Mitchell said, and the others nodded. "And you do, too."

Gideon let out a curse. "Our Pack is finally strong, and I'd hoped we would be at peace for longer than this, but I think you're right."

"Blade has never been happy with how we handled the Unveiling, and he put his contempt on the table for the Centrals becoming a Pack—as if he could stop it."

"He tried, though, and I don't think he's through with whatever plans he has," Walker said softly.

"He didn't get what he wanted with Dawn, and we killed some of his wolves." Max growled low, his brother still not fully in charge of his wolf's anger like he used to be.

"Wolves that didn't scent of Aspen," Kameron reminded them.

Dawn cleared her throat. "For a moment, I thought I scented Aspen under the witch's fire, but I could just be projecting. I thought it smelled familiar, though, like Audrey but different." His mate shook her head. "I just don't know."

"And we don't have any proof either way," Gideon growled out. "I'm meeting with the Redwoods tomorrow to discuss what we need to do to protect our own, and I think I should bring Cole into this, as well."

Three Packs with three Alphas of various strengths and experiences would make for an interesting meeting, and one Mitchell wasn't sure he wanted to miss.

"Whatever comes, though," Gideon continued, "we're not going to back down and let this happen again. We were too lax after trying to find our calm again once we gained our wards back. Never again."

"We'll find the proof," Mitchell said after a moment. "And I can't help but think that the moon goddess sent Audrey to us right now for a reason."

The others talked some more about what they needed to do for the den to keep them all on alert while Mitchell let what had happened over the past few weeks circle in his head. He *knew* Blade was behind all of this, he just couldn't prove it. And no matter how strong the Talons were, even with the help of the other Packs, they were no match for the Aspens—and no one wanted another war. What made it worse was that he wasn't even sure all of the Aspens were in on what Blade was doing. It was clear that Audrey had her misgivings about her Alpha, or maybe she was just as devious as Blade, trying to get on the Talon's good side. All Mitchell knew was that he would not let anyone else hurt his mate or his family. He'd forever have the image of his brother lying in a pool of blood in his mind, and now the sight of Dawn on the cabin floor would haunt him.

He'd make those who dared to come after his family pay.

Those that had directly hurt Dawn were already dead, and that was the only reason Mitchell was even able to sit here in this room without going wolf.

Dawn slid off his lap, and he blinked, coming back to the present rather than locked in his head. "Let's go home. Nothing can be done today, and I'm still a little tired." She sent a flare through the bond, and he knew she was just making an excuse to get him alone. And he was grateful. Considering Brandon and Walker gave him knowing looks, she hadn't quite shielded herself well when she did it. It was just one more thing he'd love teaching her about as they learned to live as mates within a Pack together. He'd never done it before, and was still feeling like a pup himself with their relationship.

They said their goodbyes, knowing this wouldn't be the last time they met with the others to discuss what to do with this new enemy that seemed to relish remaining unseen. They'd find their answers, though. Mitchell had absolute faith in his Pack and family.

Dawn tangled her fingers with his and walked by his side on their way to his—*their*—house. She had moved in the day before, and he'd shown the place to her parents and Cole. He knew he'd be spending a lot of time at the Central den these days, and he was glad of it. Anything he could do to make this easier for Dawn, he'd do. As it was, she'd quit her job at the coffee place because Gwen offered her a job at the daycare the moment she saw Dawn. And Dawn's three human friends were already planning to visit so they could get to know *this* den rather than the Centrals'. Somehow, he and Dawn were learning to mix their lives and keep who they were separately as they learned how to navigate these new waters together.

"You're lost in your thoughts again," Dawn said, tugging at his arm so they came to a stop between two large trees.

"Lots on my mind," he said simply.

She reached up and kissed his jaw before putting her hand over the mark on his shoulder where she'd sunk in her fangs the night before. They were well and truly mated, their bond healthy and growing each day. One day, they might even develop new talents from it like others who could feel emotions or even talk to one another through the bond. He'd grow with her and change over time with a mate by his side.

Part of him ached for what he lost, but when he slept with Dawn in his arms, he knew he could *live* while feeling that loss. It had taken him far too long to learn to forgive and heal, but it had taken a wolf with kind eyes and a rambling wit for him to take a chance he never thought to take.

"I love you," he said into the quiet silence. He'd never stop wanting to say that to her. He'd taken too damn long as it was.

Her eyes brightened. "I love you, too."

"And I know I told you before, but this mark,"—he put his hand on her shoulder over where he'd bitten her—"I wanted to do that *before* the cabin. I need you to know that."

She smiled at him and hugged him close. "I know. We might have been forced at the last moment, but only in timing, not desire. I'll never doubt what you feel for me. I can *feel* it in my heart and soul. How can I think anything different?"

He blew out a breath and held her tightly. Another couple walked past them and smiled. They didn't have the normal weariness in their eyes when they passed him, and he let out a rough chuckle when they were out of earshot.

"What's so funny?" Dawn asked.

"You changed me."

Her eyes widened. "Oh? How did I do that?"

"I'm not the bastard Beta of the Talons anymore. I think I've lost my edge."

She rolled her eyes, and he fake glowered at her. "Oh, shush you. Just because you smile at me doesn't mean you can't kick ass. You're still my dominant male of a mate, who is all growly and broody. Don't worry, baby, I still love your furry butt."

He snorted, shaking his head. "My butt isn't furry."

"So you say..." She laughed and tried to wiggle away as he tickled her, and he couldn't help but revel in the way their mating bond pulsed.

"Just wait until I get you home," he growled, and she licked her lips.

"Promises. Promises."

He'd thought he understood what he was walking away from when he hid from what he could have with Dawn. He had no idea.

Dawn had lived up to her name, and was indeed his new breath of life. She was everything he hadn't known he needed. She centered him and wrapped him in a sense of peace.

He'd lost a piece of himself before, but now, after taking a chance, he'd found so much more of who he could be.

And one day soon, when they faced their new enemy as one, he'd show the world who they'd messed with. Because the Talons had not only gained a new member, they'd gained a new purpose.

And they would not fail.

No matter what.

THE END

Coming Next:
Walker and Aimee

A Note from Carrie Ann

Thank you so much for reading **DESTINY DISGRACED**. I do hope if you liked this story, that you would please leave a review! Reviews help authors *and* readers.

The Talon Pack series is an on going series about the Brentwoods and their Pack. Each book is a stand alone but you can go back and start with the first book, Tattered Loyalties to see where this Pack started. The series is also set in the same world as the Redwood Pack series only thirty years later. You can read the series in any order.

Up next is all about Walker and Aimee in Eternal Mourning. These two will have their work cut out for them but I can't wait to see what happens. After that, the last two Brentwoods, Max and Kameron need their HEAs in their books as well. As for after that? Well you will just have to see! Love my paranormal romances and want more? Let the world know by reading and reviewing the Talon Pack series!

If you want to make sure you know what's coming next from me, you can sign up for my newsletter at www.CarrieAnnRyan.com; follow me on twitter at @CarrieAnnRyan, or like my Facebook page. I also have a Facebook Fan Club where we have trivia, chats, and other goodies. You guys are the reason I get to do what I do and I thank you.

Make sure you're signed up for my MAILING LIST so you can know when the next releases are available as well as find giveaways and FREE READS.

Happy Reading!

The Talon Pack:
Book 1: Tattered Loyalties
Book 2: An Alpha's Choice
Book 3: Mated in Mist
Book 4: Wolf Betrayed
Book 5: Fractured Silence
Book 6: Destiny Disgraced
Book 7: Eternal Mourning (Coming Feb 2018)
Book 8: Strength Enduring (Coming July 2018)

Want to keep up to date with the next Carrie Ann
Ryan Release? Receive Text Alerts easily!
Text CARRIE to 24587

About Carrie Ann

Carrie Ann Ryan is the New York Times and USA Today bestselling author of contemporary and paranormal romance. Her works include the Montgomery Ink, Redwood Pack, Talon Pack, and Gallagher Brothers series, which have sold over 2.0 million books worldwide. She started writing while in graduate school for her advanced degree in chemistry and hasn't stopped since. Carrie Ann has written over fifty novels and novellas with more in the works. When she's not writing about bearded tattooed men or alpha wolves that need to find their mates, she's reading as much as she can and exploring the world of baking and gourmet cooking.

www.CarrieAnnRyan.com

More from Carrie Ann

Montgomery Ink:
Book 0.5: Ink Inspired
Book 0.6: Ink Reunited
Book 1: Delicate Ink
The Montgomery Ink Box Set (Contains Books 0.5, 0.6, 1)
Book 1.5: Forever Ink
Book 2: Tempting Boundaries
Book 3: Harder than Words
Book 4: Written in Ink
Book 4.5: Hidden Ink
Book 5: Ink Enduring
Book 6: Ink Exposed
Book 6.5: Adoring Ink
Book 6.6: Love, Honor, & Ink
Book 7: Inked Expressions
Book 8: Inked Memories (Coming Oct 2017)

Montgomery Ink: Colorado Springs
Book 1: Fallen Ink (Coming Apr 2018)

The Gallagher Brothers Series:
A Montgomery Ink Spin Off Series
Book 1: Love Restored
Book 2: Passion Restored
Book 3: Hope Restored

The Whiskey and Lies Series:
A Montgomery Ink Spin Off Series
Book 1: Whiskey Secrets (Coming Jan 2018)
Book 2: Whiskey Reveals (Coming June 2018)

The Talon Pack:
Book 1: Tattered Loyalties
Book 2: An Alpha's Choice
Book 3: Mated in Mist
Book 4: Wolf Betrayed
Book 5: Fractured Silence
Book 6: Destiny Disgraced
Book 7: Eternal Mourning (Coming Feb 2018)
Book 8: Strength Enduring (Coming July 2018)

Redwood Pack Series:
Book 1: An Alpha's Path
Book 2: A Taste for a Mate
Book 3: Trinity Bound
Redwood Pack Box Set (Contains Books 1-3)
Book 3.5: A Night Away
Book 4: Enforcer's Redemption
Book 4.5: Blurred Expectations
Book 4.7: Forgiveness
Book 5: Shattered Emotions
Book 6: Hidden Destiny
Book 6.5: A Beta's Haven
Book 7: Fighting Fate
Book 7.5: Loving the Omega
Book 7.7: The Hunted Heart
Book 8: Wicked Wolf
The Complete Redwood Pack Box Set (Contains Books 1-7.7)

The Branded Pack Series:
(Written with Alexandra Ivy)
Book 1: Stolen and Forgiven
Book 2: Abandoned and Unseen
Book 3: Buried and Shadowed

Dante's Circle Series:

Book 1: Dust of My Wings
Book 2: Her Warriors' Three Wishes
Book 3: An Unlucky Moon
The Dante's Circle Box Set (Contains Books 1-3)
Book 3.5: His Choice
Book 4: Tangled Innocence
Book 5: Fierce Enchantment
Book 6: An Immortal's Song
Book 7: Prowled Darkness
The Complete Dante's Circle Series (Contains Books 1-7)

Holiday, Montana Series:
Book 1: Charmed Spirits
Book 2: Santa's Executive
Book 3: Finding Abigail
The Holiday, Montana Box Set (Contains Books 1-3)
Book 4: Her Lucky Love
Book 5: Dreams of Ivory
The Complete Holiday, Montana Box Set (Contains Books 1-5)

Stand Alone Romances:
Finally Found You
Flame and Ink
Ink Ever After
Dropout

Delicate Ink

"If you don't turn that fucking music down, I'm going to ram this tattoo gun up a place no one on this earth should ever see."

Austin Montgomery lifted the needle from his client's arm so he could hold back a rough chuckle. He let his foot slide off the pedal so he could keep his composure. Dear Lord, his sister Maya clearly needed more coffee in her life.

Or for someone to turn down the fucking music in the shop.

"You're not even working, Maya. Let me have my tunes," Sloane, another artist, mumbled under his breath. Yeah, he didn't yell it. Didn't need to. No one wanted to yell at Austin's sister. The man might be as big as a house and made of pure muscle, but no one messed with Maya.

Not if they wanted to live.

"I'm sketching, you dumbass," Maya sniped, even though the smile in her eyes belied her wrath. His sister loved Sloane like a brother. Not that she didn't have enough brothers and sisters to begin with, but the Montgomerys always had their arms open for strays and spares.

Austin rolled his eyes at the pair's antics and stood up from his stool, his body aching from being bent over for too long. He refrained from saying that aloud as Maya and Sloane would have a joke for that. He usually preferred to have the other person in bed— or in the kitchen, office, doorway, etc—bent over, but that wasn't where he would allow his mind to go. As it was, he was too damn old to be sitting in that position for too long, but he wanted to get this sleeve done for his customer.

"Hold on a sec, Rick," he said to the man in the chair. "Want juice or anything? I'm going to stretch my legs and make sure Maya doesn't kill Sloane." He winked as he said it, just in case his client didn't get the joke.

People could be so touchy when siblings threatened each other with bodily harm even while they smiled as they said it.

"Juice sounds good," Rick slurred, a sappy smile on his face. "Don't let Maya kill you."

Rick blinked his eyes open, the adrenaline running through his system giving him the high that a few patrons got once they were in the chair for a couple hours. To Austin, there was nothing better than having Maya ink his skin—or doing it himself— and letting the needle do its work. He wasn't a pain junkie, far from it if he was honest with himself, but he liked the adrenaline that led the way into fucking fantastic art. While some people thought bodies were sacred and tattoos only marred them, he knew it differently. Art on canvas, any canvas, could have the potential to be art worth bleeding for. As such, he was particular as to who laid a needle on his skin. He only let Maya ink him when he couldn't do it himself. Maya was the same way. Whatever she couldn't do herself, he did.

They were brother and sister, friends, and co-owners of Montgomery Ink.

He and Maya had opened the shop a decade ago when she'd turned twenty. He probably could have opened it a few years earlier since he was eight years older than Maya, but he'd wanted to wait until she was ready. They were joint owners. It had never been his shop while she worked with him. They both had equal say, although with the way Maya spoke, sometimes her voice seemed louder. His deeper one carried just as much weight, even if he didn't yell as much.

Barely.

Sure, he wasn't as loud as Maya, but he got his point across when needed. His voice held control and authority.

He picked up a juice box for Rick from their mini-fridge and turned down the music on his way back. Sloane scowled at him, but the corner of his mouth twitched as if he held back a laugh.

"Thank God one of you has a brain in his head," Maya mumbled in the now quieter room. She rolled her eyes as both he and Sloane flipped her off then went back to her sketch. Yeah, she could have gotten up to turn the music down herself, but then she couldn't have vented her excess energy at the two of them. That was just how his sister worked, and there would be no changing that.

He went back to his station situated in the back so he had the corner space, handed Rick his juice, then rubbed his back. Damn, he was getting old. Thirty-eight wasn't that far up there on the scales, but ever since he'd gotten back from New Orleans, he hadn't been able to shake the weight of something off of his chest.

He needed to be honest. He'd started feeling this way since before New Orleans. He'd gone down to the city to visit his cousin Shep and try to get out of his funk. He'd broken up with Shannon right before then; however, in reality, it wasn't as much a breakup as a lack of connection and communication. They hadn't cared about each other enough to move on to the next level, and as sad as that was, he was fine with it. If he couldn't get up the energy to pursue a woman beyond a couple of weeks or months of heat, then he knew he was the problem. He just didn't know the solution. Shannon hadn't been the first woman who had ended the relationship in that fashion. There'd been Brenda, Sandrine, and another one named Maggie.

He'd cared for all of them at the time. He wasn't a complete asshole, but he'd known deep down that they weren't going to be with him forever, and they thought the same of him. He also knew that it was time to actually find a woman to settle down with. If he wanted a future, a family, he was running out of time.

Going to New Orleans hadn't worked out in the least considering, at the time, Shep was falling in love with a pretty blonde named Shea. Not that Austin begrudged the man that. Shep had been his best friend growing up, closer to him than his four brothers and three sisters. It'd helped that he and Shep were the same age while the next of his siblings, the twins Storm and Wes, were four years younger.

His parents had taken their time to have eight kids, meaning he was a full fifteen years older than the baby, Miranda, but he hadn't cared. The eight of them, most of his cousins, and a few strays were as close as ever. He'd helped raise the youngest ones as an older brother but had never felt like he had to. His parents, Marie and Harry, loved each of their kids equally and had put their whole beings into their roles as parents. Every single concert, game, ceremony, or even parent-teacher meeting was attended by at least one of them. On the good days, the ones where Dad could get off work and Mom had the day off from Montgomery Inc., they both would attend. They loved their kids.

He loved being a Montgomery.

The sound of Sloane's needle buzzing as he sang whatever tune played in his head made Austin grin.

And he fucking *loved* his shop.

Every bare brick and block of polished wood, every splash of black and hot pink—colors he and Maya had fought on and he'd eventually given in to—made him feel at home. He'd taken the family crest and symbol, the large MI surrounded by a broken floral circle, and used it as their logo. His brothers, Storm and Wes, owned Montgomery Inc., a family construction company that their father had once owned and where their mother had worked at his side before they'd retired. They, too, used the same logo since it meant family to them.

In fact, the MI was tattooed on every single immediate family member—including his parents. His own was on his right forearm tangled in the rest of his sleeve but given a place of meaning. It meant Montgomery Iris—*open your eyes, see the beauty, remember who you are*. It was only natural to use it for their two respective companies.

Not that the Ink vs Inc. wasn't confusing as hell, but fuck, they were Montgomerys. They could do whatever they wanted. As long as they were together, they'd get through it.

Montgomery Ink was just as much his home as his house on the ravine. While Shep had gone on to work at Midnight Ink and created another family there, Austin had always wanted to own his shop. Maya growing up to want to do the same thing had only helped.

Montgomery Ink was now a thriving business in downtown Denver right off 16th Street Mall. They were near parking, food, and coffee. There really wasn't more he needed. The drive in most mornings could suck once he got on I-25, but it was worth it to live out in Arvada. The 'burbs around Denver made it easy to live in one area of the city and work in another. Commutes, though hellish at rush hour, weren't as bad as some. This way he got the city living when it came to work and play, and the option to hide behind the trees pressed up against the foothills of the Rocky Mountains once he got home.

It was the best of both worlds.

At least for him.

Austin got back on his stool and concentrated on Rick's sleeve for another hour before calling it quits. He needed a break for his lower back, and Rick needed a break from the pain. Not that Rick was feeling much since the man currently looked like he'd just gotten laid—pain freaks, Austin loved them—but he didn't want to push either of them too far. Also, Plus Rick's arm had started to swell slightly from all the shading and multiple colors. They'd do another session, the last, hopefully, in a month or so when both of them could work it in their schedules and then finish up.

Austin scowled at the computer at the front of shop, his fingers too big for the damn keys on the prissy computer Maya had demanded they buy.

"Fuck!"

He'd just deleted Rick's whole account because he couldn't find the right button.

"Maya, get your ass over here and fix this. I don't know what the hell I did."

Maya lifted one pierced brow as she worked on a lower back tattoo for some teenage girl who didn't look old enough to get ink in the first place.

"I'm busy, Austin. You're not an idiot, though evidence at the moment points to the contrary. Fix it yourself. I can't help it if you have ape hands."

Austin flipped her off then took a sip of his Coke, wishing he had something stronger considering he hated paperwork. "I was fine with the old keyboard and the PC, Maya. You're the one who wanted to go with the Mac because it looked pretty."

"Fuck you, Austin. I wanted a Mac because I like the software."

Austin snorted while trying to figure out how to find Rick's file. He was pretty sure it was a lost cause at this point. "You hate the software as much as I do. You hit the damn red X and close out files more than I do. Everything's in the wrong place, and the keyboard is way too fucking dainty."

"I'm going to go with Austin on this one," Sloane added in, his beefy hands in the air.

"See? I'm not alone."

Maya let out a breath. "We can get another keyboard for you and Gigantor's hands, but we need to keep the Mac."

"And why is that?" he demanded.

"Because we just spent a whole lot of money on it, and once it goes, we can get another PC. Fuck the idea that everything can be all in one. I can't figure it out either." She held up a hand. "And don't even think about breaking it. I'll know, Austin. I *always* know."

Austin held back a grin. He wouldn't be surprised if the computer met with an earlier than expected unfortunate fate now that Maya had relented.

Right then, however, that idea didn't help. He needed to find Rick's file.

"Callie!" Austin yelled over the buzz of needles and soft music Maya had allowed them to play.

"What?" His apprentice came out of the break room, a sketchbook in one hand and a smirk on her face. She'd dyed her hair again so it had black and red highlights. It looked good on her, but honestly, he never knew what color she'd have next. "Break something on the computer again with those big man hands?"

"Shut up, minion," he teased. Callie was an up-and-coming artist, and if she kept on the track she was on, he and Maya knew she'd be getting her own chair at Montgomery Ink soon. Not that he'd tell Callie that, though. He liked keeping her on her toes. She reminded him of his little sister Miranda so much that he couldn't help but treat her as such.

She pushed him out of the way and groaned. "Did you have to press *every* button as you rampaged through the operating system?"

Austin could have sworn he felt his cheeks heat, but since he had a thick enough beard, he knew no one would have been able to tell.

Hopefully.

He hated feeling as if he didn't know what he was doing. It wasn't as if he didn't know how to use a computer. He wasn't an idiot. He just didn't know *this* computer. And it bugged the shit out of him.

After a couple of keystrokes and a click of the mouse, Callie stepped back with a smug smile on her face. "Okay, boss, you're all ready to go, and Rick's file is back where it should be. What else do you need from me?"

He bopped her on the head, messing up her red and black hair he knew she spent an hour on every morning with a flat iron. He couldn't help it.

"Go clean a toilet or something."

Callie rolled her eyes. "I'm going to go sketch. And you're welcome."

"Thanks for fixing the damn thing. And really, go clean the bathroom."

"Not gonna do it," she sang as she skipped to the break room.

"You really have no control over your apprentice," Sloane commented from his station.

Because he didn't want that type of control with her. Well, hell, his mind kept going to that dark place every few minutes it seemed.

"Shut up, asshole."

"I see your vocabulary hasn't changed much," Shannon purred from the doorway.

He closed his eyes and prayed for patience. Okay, maybe he'd lied to himself when he said it was mutual and easy to break up with her. The damn woman kept showing up. He didn't think she wanted him, but she didn't want him to forget her either.

He did not understand women.

Especially this one.

"What do you want, Shannon?" he bit out, needing that drink now more than ever.

She sauntered over to him and scraped her long, red nail down his chest. He'd liked that once. Now, not even a little. They were decent together when they'd dated, but he'd had to hide most of himself from her. She'd never tasted the edge of his flogger or felt his hand on her ass when she'd been bent over his lap. That hadn't been what she wanted, and Austin was into the kind of kink that meant he wanted what he wanted when he wanted. It didn't mean he wanted it every time.

Not that Shannon would ever understand that.

"Oh, baby, you know what I want."

He barely resisted the urge to roll his eyes. As he took a step back, he saw the gleam in her eyes and decided to head it off at the pass. He was in no mood to play her games, or whatever she wanted to do that night. He wanted to go home, drink a beer, and forget this oddly annoying day.

"If you don't want ink, then I don't know what you're doing here, Shannon. We're done." He tried to say it quietly, but his voice was deep, and it carried.

"How could you be so cruel?" She pouted.

"Oh, for the love of God," Maya sneered. "Go home, little girl. You and Austin are through, and I'm pretty sure it was mutual. Oh, and you're not getting any ink here. You're not getting Austin's hands on you this way, and there's no way in hell I'm putting my art on you. Not if you keep coming back to bug the man you didn't really date in the first place."

"Bi—" Shannon cut herself off as Austin glared. Nobody called his sister a bitch. Nobody.

"Goodbye, Shannon." Jesus, he was too old for this shit.

"Fine. I see how it is. Whatever. You were only an okay lay anyway." She shook her ass as she left, bumping into a woman in a linen skirt and blouse.

The woman, whose long honey-brown hair hung in waves down to her breasts, raised a brow. "I see your business has an...interesting clientele."

Austin clenched his jaw. Seriously the wrong thing to say after Shannon.

"If you've got a problem, you can head on right back to where you came from, Legs," he bit out, his voice harsher than he'd intended.

She stiffened then raised her chin, a clear sense of disdain radiating off of her.

Oh yes, he knew who this was, legs and all. Ms. Elder. He hadn't caught a first name. Hadn't wanted to. She had to be in her late twenties, maybe, and owned the soon-to-be-opened boutique across the street. He'd seen her strut around in her too-tall heels and short skirts but hadn't been formally introduced.

Not that he wanted an introduction.

She was too damn stuffy and ritzy for his taste. Not only her store but the woman herself. The look of disdain on her face made him want to show her the door and never let her back in.

He knew what he looked like. Longish dark brown hair, thick beard, muscles covered in ink with a hint of more ink coming out of his shirt. He looked like a felon to some people who didn't know the difference, though he'd never seen the inside of a jail cell in his life. But he knew people like Ms. Elder. They judged people like him. And that one eyebrow pissed him the fuck off.

He didn't want this woman's boutique across the street from him. He'd liked it when it was an old record store. People didn't glare at his store that way. Now he had to walk past the mannequins with the rich clothes and tiny lacy scraps of things if he wanted a fucking coffee from the shop next door.

Damn it, this woman pissed him off, and he had no idea why.

"Nice to meet you too. Callie!" he shouted, his eyes still on Ms. Elder as if he couldn't pull his gaze from her. Her green eyes never left his either, and the uncomfortable feeling in his gut wouldn't go away.

Callie ran up beside him and held out her hand. "Hi, I'm Callie. How can I help you?"

Ms. Elder blinked once. Twice. "I think I made a mistake," she whispered.

Fuck. Now he felt like a heel. He didn't know what it was with this woman, but he couldn't help but act like an ass. She hadn't even done anything but lift an eyebrow at him, and he'd already set out to hate her.

Callie shook her head then reached for Ms. Elder's elbow. "I'm sure you haven't. Ignore the growly, bearded man over there. He needs more caffeine. And his ex was just in here; that alone would make anyone want to jump off the Royal Gorge. So, tell me, how can I help you? Oh! And what's your name?"

Ms. Elder followed Callie to the sitting area with leather couches and portfolios spread over the coffee table and then sat down.

"I'm Sierra, and I want a tattoo." She looked over her shoulder and glared at Austin. "Or, at least, I thought I did."

Austin held back a wince when she turned her attention from him and cursed himself. Well, fuck. He needed to learn not to put his foot in his mouth, but damn it, how was he supposed to know she wanted a tattoo? For all he knew, she wanted to come in there and look down on the place. That was his own prejudice coming into play. He needed to make it up to her. After all, they were neighbors now. However, from the cross look on her face and the feeling in the room, he knew that he wasn't going to be able to make it up to her today. He'd let Callie help her out to start with, and then he'd make sure he was the one who laid ink on her skin.

After all, it was the least he could do. Besides, his hands all of a sudden—or not so suddenly if he really thought about it—wanted to touch that delicate skin of hers and find out her secrets.

Austin cursed. He wouldn't let his thoughts go down that path. She'd break under his care, under his needs. Sure, Sierra Elder might be hot, but she wasn't the woman for him.

If he knew anything, he knew *that* for sure.

Love Restored

In the first of a Montgomery Ink spin-off series from NYT Bestselling Author Carrie Ann Ryan, a broken man uncovers the truth of what it means to take a second chance with the most unexpected woman...

Graham Gallagher has seen it all. And when tragedy struck, lost it all. He's been the backbone of his brothers, the one they all rely on in their lives and business. And when it comes to falling in love and creating a life, he knows what it's like to have it all and watch it crumble. He's done with looking for another person to warm his bed, but apparently he didn't learn his lesson because the new piercer at Montgomery Ink tempts him like no other.

Blake Brennen may have been born a trust fund baby, but she's created a whole new life for herself in the world of ink, piercings, and freedom. Only the ties she'd thought she'd cut long ago aren't as severed as she'd believed. When she finds Graham constantly in her path, she knows from first glance that he's the wrong kind of guy for her. Except that Blake excels at making the wrong choice and Graham might be the ultimate temptation for the bad girl she'd thought long buried.

Tattered Loyalties

When the great war between the Redwoods and the Centrals occurred three decades ago, the Talon Pack risked their lives for the side of good. After tragedy struck, Gideon Brentwood became the Alpha of the Talons. But the Pack's stability is threatened, and he's forced to take mate—only the one fate puts in his path is the woman he shouldn't want.

Though the daughter of the Redwood Pack's Beta, Brie Jamenson has known peace for most of her life. When she finds the man who could be her mate, she's shocked to discover Gideon is the Alpha wolf of the Talon Pack. As a submissive, her strength lies in her heart, not her claws. But if her new Pack disagrees or disapproves, the consequences could be fatal.

As the worlds Brie and Gideon have always known begin to shift, they must face their challenges together in order to help their Pack and seal their bond. But when the Pack is threatened from the inside, Gideon doesn't know who he can trust and Brie's life could be forfeit in the crossfire. It will take the strength of an Alpha and the courage of his mate to realize where true loyalties lie.

7503

67252464R00146

Made in the USA
Lexington, KY
10 September 2017